Bella

R. M. Francis

Dear Alison,
Thanks so much!

Wild Pressed Books

Editor: Tracey Scott-Townsend

Cover Art and Design by Tracey Scott-Townsend

ISBN: 978-1-9164896-4-6

Published by Wild Pressed Books: 2020

Wild Pressed Books, UK Business Reg. No. 09550738

http://www.wildpressedbooks.com

For the restless ghosts of the Black Country and my uber-wenches, Gemma and Elsbeth.

Foreword

by Anthony Cartwright

I think everyone who grows up in the Black Country one day asks themselves, in one way or another, *Who Put Bella Down the Wych-Elm?* The enigmatic strangeness of the question, literal and metaphoric, seems to represent some half-hidden truth about the place and the people. R. M. Francis's Bella is a kind of Black Country folk-horror, a re-imagining of the very real tragedy, itself become something like myth.

The story is told as if a set of characters, a babble of voices, suddenly entered a George Shaw landscape - Midland, Edgeland, Gothic - living lives among the streets of terraced houses and estates between "places that are not even towns" and on the edge of even more in-between places, where the Wych-Elm grows. But the most important thing is how the voices we hear seem somehow both central to a culture (English, Industrial, Midland) and marginalised by it (whether by sexuality, gender, background, religion, the collapse

v

of industry). Thus Timothy Carmody - gay, Irish, Catholic, English, Black Country hard man and victim all at the same time - and all the other complex characters within. This sense of the in-between, of the weird and the eerie, as Mark Fisher would have it, in both the people and place it depicts, is the great triumph of this novel.

Bella

You call me Bella. I am always here, lurking. I am just out of sight. Just out of reach. I am the mar. I am the foxy infraction. Never living, never dead. A shade that germs into and out of you.

1

Michelle

I doh believe in witches or ghosts or whatnot, but there was summat about Saltwells and Bella, in one form or another, 'er was always theya. Tim said 'e was an atheist but 'e still day walk under ladders an' 'e 'ated black cats. Iss the same wi' Bella, even if you think iss just a story, you still doh wanna test it. Tim said 'e knew wharr 'ad 'appened.

I needed to know.

I remember drivin' up from The Delph towards Cradley, an' we were stopped at the lights at the top 'a Quarry Bank. Tony was with me an' 'e'd pointed it out. Iss a crossroads 'ere an' iss all concrete, brick, tarmac. Iss grey, cold an' stoney. Back in the day they'd mek nails an' chain if ya went down one road, an' they'd mek glass if you turned around. Most 'a that 'ad died

3

out so it was just a shadow of a place. A junction just to get to somewhere else. The lights at Quarry Bank am four-way with three lanes at each openin', iss busy wi' people headin' to the shops, to work, iss always busy an' ya never gerr'across, you've always gorra wait. It ay nothin' 'cept a border between a couple 'a places that ay proper towns anyroad. Tony was wi' me an' 'e sid it.

See, 'round 'ere weem always lookin' back. Weem built from what come before us. Chains, steel, nails. Soot an' smoke in the skies. Most of iss gone now. We've still got red bricks an' concrete, corrugated metal an' all that. But we ay got forges. We ay got mystic blacksmiths. We've got almost-barren high streets. We've got slick, glass, brass an' plastic we've built over the works with – stockin' rows 'a dead 'eaded credit controllers, PPI reps, retail consultants. We've got Merry Hill – an indoor town that spreads out in sanitised pound-zones. Then there's what's left-over. Little dry suburbs that sink between 'ills, where dead factories am wrapped in weeds, an' big 'ousin' estates, all wet an' grey, an' all punctured in electric light – them no go zones unless you'm from theya – each zone 'as iss own 'alf deserted Labour club, iss own brand 'a menacin' teen, iss own birr'a cut or brook or strange patch 'a green land that mopes between a terrace row an' the mechanic's.

Tony was wi' me an' 'e sid it.

Pokin' out through a crack in the curb was a thin, green vine, an' on the vine were tiny green tomatoes.

4

Tony said it was like Detroit, 'ow it was once the biggest industrial hub in the US,'ow nature 'ad started to claim back the city now it'd run iss course. There was summat frightnin' about that: it come out 'a the ground, thass what them meant to do, but the ground was meant to be controlled by us, not weeds. I wondered what else was lurkin' under our industry, waitin' to come back. It med me think of Saltwells an' where wid play when we was kids.

Who put Bella down the Wych-Elm?

It was everywhere – this tag. Chalked up over the red and grey bricks on our estate. This question – this warning. Most of us 'ad got used to it. Just walked past the signs on the Wrenna, down Cinder Bank or Lodge 'ill, like it was just another daily blot on a daily-blotted place.

Bella was a wench who'd bin found in Saltwells one night, 'er was. 'Er was dead – just bones. Er'd bin stashed theya donkeys agoo and no one 'ad ever found out how. So a bunch on 'um 'ad started paintin' it up on the walls of old factories – *Who put Bella down the Wych-Elm?*

When I sez donkeys agoo, I mean before the steelworks closed and before busses stopped comin' through and before job shop queues. It wor non 'a our lot, it was before they'd built houses on the Sledmere. Nan 'ad said it went back to when they was kids in the fifties. Some on 'em, the old 'uns in Turner's, 'ud say it was saft – just a local story dads'd use to shut the kids up. But some on 'em, some said it happened just like

5

the story said it 'ad.

After a night 'a suppin' in the pub, one 'a them old sorts boat men and tinkers used – not like Turner's or The 'Ope where wid sink shit-tasting shots and bark along to Karaoke tracks – an old one like Pardoe's with wood an' brass an' open fires: Bella 'ad 'ad 'er fill an' stumbled home. 'Er must 'a got lost 'cause 'er ended up facin' the wrong way in Saltwells, and maybe 'er was followed and maybe 'er'd pissed someone off, or maybe 'er fancied a bit 'a one 'a the scrap men or somethin', 'cause 'er wor alone. Whoever 'ad bin wi 'er an' whyever they'd bin theya we doh know. We just know the'd fucked 'er, took a stone or summat to 'er yed an' cut 'er up.

Years later, a few kids from Derby End Scouts 'ad gone out trackin' or somethin' an' they'd looked inside this big old tree. A Wych-Elm. Iss still theya too.

Most 'a Saltwells is thin, light coloured trees an' bushes, there's bigguns too but not like the Wych-Elm. Most 'a Saltwells is paths, an' it would 'a bin back in the fifties, I reckon. You can follow the paths down the quarry an' through the bluebells an' you wouln't 'a thought you was still in Netherton, with all the greens an' browns an' the almost quiet. You gorra know where to find the Wych-Elm. It 'ay on the paths. You cut through a thicket up by where it meets the Res an' you follow the skinny route med out 'a the bits 'a broken ground med by the few broken sorts who went lookin'. The Wych-Elm sorta sits in a circle, where nothin' else grows around it. It 'ay tall, but iss fat. Iss dark an'

6

leafless an' brittle an' iss gorra big laceration down the front – thass where they'd found 'er. Them Scouts looked inside an' pulled out 'er cracked-up skull. Then the police found bits 'a old shoes an' cloth an' a few other bones around the circle 'a ground. But it'd bin too long and no one knew who'd bin theya or why or nothin'. So the funny fuckers 'round 'eya starting writing *Who put Bella down the Wych Elm?* on all the walls.

I doh even know where the name Bella comes from.

'Er gets under our skin too, Bella does. Like the tomatoes finding roots in cracked concrete.

———————

Tim 'ad bin about thirteen. His family 'ad moved to the Sledmere when 'e was ten. At the beginning 'a the eighties they'd bought their council house down Lodge 'ill, 'is Dad built a porch and med a drive where the front lawn was. 'E knew people who'd get stuff on the cheap and e'd fix anything. They sold up and now had a spot down 'ere. 'E wor a normal lad, Tim. Not dangerous but not the sem as the other lads on the estate. Always on 'es own, 'e was. Every now an' then you'd see 'im ferritin' about. He'd be iverin' about in the bushes that separated our houses an' the cut. We'd be on the benches an' the walls, smokin' fags an' loffin' at the lads who tried to chuck bibbles off the yeds 'a geese. No one knew what 'e was up to. The lads 'ated 'im, but knew his Dad'd fuck 'em up if anythin' 'appened. Me an' Gem knew 'is mom, 'er worked with

7

Nan, we day wanta be 'is mate but we day wanta pick on 'im either. 'E was odd, Tim. Not dangerous, but not the sem as us.

Early on at school there was times when 'e'd try an' fit in, burr'e was crap arr'it. Jay an' Sam was 'oldin' forth by the sports 'all. Thass where we all hung out on break. Tim an' 'is lot hung on the steps next to it. They was always on the edge of it.

"My old mon's gorra CD player," Jay said. "'E's got ten CDs, iss bostin'."

We day think CDs'd last then. Me an' Gem taped stuff off the radio.

"Wass wrong wi' tapes an' records?" Gem asked. "It all works anyroad. Yo' cor tape CDs can yo'?"

Then Tim cries over, "the mind is like an umbrella. It's most useful when open."

We loffed our 'eads off. Tim was called Brolley for about a year. *Ay Brolley, yo' wanker!* Thass when it started really. 'E was alright, we just found a gap.

'E day do 'imself any favours neither. In science one day the lads was tekkin' the piss an' 'is response was:

"Finished my job at the umbrella factory ... I was only covering for someone."

That day do 'im any favours. 'E tried it again a few times.

"Whatcha call a parrot wi' an umbrella? Polly unsaturated."

Thass warr'e was to us. Someone who'd say weird stuff. Someone you'd see werritin' about in the bushes.

8

'E told me years later. We'd gone to the re-opening of The Bell in Stourbridge an' 'e got me a drink and we stayed in touch after that. 'E told me e'd bin wankin'. E'd bin obsessed with it back then. Said he couln't 'a done it at home 'cause 'e's Dad used to slap 'is mom when someone kissed on *Neighbours* or *Corrie* an' 'er day look away, so 'e'd 'a bin missin' limbs if 'is Dad 'ad sin him bein' a sinner. So 'e 'ad to goo outta the house, but not where the other kids were. Mebe thass why. Ya 'ear about it, doh ya? About people who cor do summat, so it meks 'em wuss fer doin' it. 'Iss that old thing about seein' a sign like doh walk on the grass, or summat, an' then y'am compelled to do it, even though ya day even think about it before.

Stourbridge was the posh side, really. Yo'd end up in more fights on the high street theya, 'cause the posh kids couln't 'andle theya ale an' they could afford to tek coke, an' thass a shit cocktail wi' dick'eads. But they had farmer's markets an' Waitrose, craft beers an' poetry nights an' all that. Tim loved that stuff. They re-opened The Bell as a gay bar. That was a big deal 'round 'ere. Me an' our Gem went to the openin' an' thass where we sid Tim. The place was packed. Coloured lights flashin' an' music pumpin' out. Took us about fifteen minutes each time at the bar. Thass where we sid Tim. Me an' Gem was sat at a table by the bar an' through the rabble I sid a lanky bloke starin' at us. 'E 'ad a white shirt on, black trousers an' a black waistcoat. 'E stood out. Just stood theya starin'. 'E took a couple 'a steps towards us. I thought

9

I was gonna 'av to get cute with 'im.

"Thass Brolley! Thass Tim Carmody, ay it?" Gem said. It was. 'E strutted over to us. Starin'.

"We ay interested," I said. That was before Gem clocked 'im. "I gerr 'er drinks," pointin' at our Gem. "An' 'er gess mine."

"No chance of a drink with an old school mate then?" 'E said.

Thass when our Gem clocked 'im. We loffed. 'E gorr'us a drink. Thass where 'e started tellin' us about Saltwells, an' Bella an' 'is weird habits.

Me an' Tim stayed in touch. I had to find out. I needed it. We'd meet up at The Fox and Grapes or The Red Crow. No one knew us up theya. 'E said 'e knew about Bella.

Stan

Bella stories 'ave bin abaart since the 1950s, ay they, mebe earlier than that. Saltwells an' Bella an' all that gerr under our skin 'ere, they do. Like 'er's on the edge of us. Everyone's gorra story. Most am Billy bullshitters, ay they.

Our Michelle's different though, ay 'er. Me an' 'er Nan 'ave looked after 'er since 'er was a bab. 'Er dad's inside an' her mom's jed. Thass all arm tellin'. D'ya get me?

Now, the night 'er dad, my own son, got took in by the coppers, our Michelle, only three, 'er was, 'er went

10

missin', day 'er. 'Er gorr out somehow. Found 'er way down Lodge 'ill an' med 'er way into Saltwells, day 'er.

We doh know wharr 'appened but they'd found 'er out in Saltwells woods. At the Wych-Elm, in tears. Screamin' an' blartin', 'er was, wor 'er. 'Er was in shock, they said. Took 'er nan abaart three hours to calm 'er down an' I 'ad te sup six pints, before I did, day I.

Te this day, no one knows wharr 'appened. 'Ow did 'er get out? Why did 'er goo te the Wych-Elm? Te this day, no one knows.

Me and' 'er nan 'ave promised te not tell 'er a thing, ay we. We'll play along with the stories an' whatnot but 'er wo' 'ear the truth 'a that night an 'er wo 'ear what 'er old mon did te 'er mom. 'Er nan enjoys 'erself with it – 'er meks fun out 'a tales, doh 'er. I'll just stay quiet. Bella gets te all of us in some way, though, doh 'er.

Our Michelle's different though, ay 'er. You'll 'ear 'er say *I need to know an' I've gorra find out*, 'er'll say. We all know the stories, doh we. 'Er wants to figure it out proper, 'er does. You'll 'ear 'er talkin' to the wench in Turner's an' the old blokes who used to bait the woods. 'Er never less it goo, 'er doh. Like there's a trace from that night thass infected 'er, ay it.

Tim

Honestly, I used to go into the line of trees and bushes between the estate an' the cut. It seemed safe, like, there wor no paths, like or nothin'. Honestly, you could tell people 'ad been there from bits of litter an' the odd bit of clothin' left by a tramp. I found a spot that you could just about get one body into, like, get down on my knees, like, pull open a few pages of porno an' toss off. It only ever took a few minutes, like. It was safer in there but there was summat about bein' outside too. Honestly, I liked bein' close to home, bein' unseen, like, but close to bein' seen.

I think I was okay an' not okay back then. I was alright on my own an' I day really need loads of muckers an' all that like. But, you know, honestly, school sort of does strange stuff to us, doh it? The cool guys like Jay an' Sam would all be cantin' about sex an' stuff an', like, there was part of me that wanted to measure up to that too.

We was different. We was from Lodge 'ill an' even though that's just on the end of Netherton, like, it's still not Sledmere. The other thing was my Dad an' our Irish blood an' the catholic shit. Honestly, all that, an' the talk at school, got me wankin'. It'd got quite bad towards the back end of that summer. I was desperate to get laid. I must've been about thirteen or fourteen and I'd go out in the mornin' and toss off, then again after lunch and before it got dark. It was a habit like. I just got through most of the day an' measured it out in wanks, to be honest.

I had a stash of pornos I'd found down by the Dudley Tunnel but by the end of summer it'd all gone stale, like. I dunno if kids find pornos these days. We doh really have the same spaces for 'em, to be honest. I was desperate to get laid. Thass why I did it, like. Thass why I went to Nicki.

See, I had a couple of mates, Rich and Dave, but we spent all our time talkin' about Gary Newman an', Jem an' the holograms, like, playin' with our Wackywall walkers. We'd race 'em down the sports'all windows. Honestly, I couldn't talk about stuff like this with them until a few years on, an' even then it was different. But I was obsessed with it. It had to be outside. It had to be often. Then, it grows, like. It grew. I had to get laid. Thass why I went to Nicki.

I didn't know what I was doing or what I wanted at first, like. It started with the wankin', moved on to the porn – I had to collect it, then I started tekkin' bits of fruit down the bushes with me. Mom's Cantaloupe, like.

At first I had to come up with a plan to get over there. I decided to get Dad's lawnmower and pretend I was gonna make some pocket money around the estate. They were happy with this to be honest.

"E's got your spirit, Carrick, ay 'e", Mom 'ad said.

Now, you cor just knock on one door, get laid and then give up the game, so I thought I'd start on my street first and work around to Nicki's. Mowed about ten fuckin' lawns before I got to hers. Everyone kept sayin', like, Ah, iss Carrick's kid, goo on then, Bab. I gee yer a quid.

I 'ad to cut the wankin' down big time, like.

Honestly, I did three lawns a day. 'Round about. Then got to Nicki. That old wench had me do front an' back. She had me do what Mick shoulda done before it

13

started, to be honest.

As soon as she opened the door she knew what was happenin' – I knew an' she knew an' we still had to go through the motions. Wust fuckin' foreplay I've ever add, like.

Honestly, it was boilin' that summer. An' her lawn was massive. Took ages. I could feel her lookin' over me as I worked. Even that got me up a little, like.

"You look like you need a squash," she said to me.

So I went in an' had a squash. There she was, honestly, dressed in her fake silk robe, like, sittin' me down at the table, touchin' my shoulders for a moment too much as she led me, leanin' over me as she placed the tumbler down. Eyelashes flickerin', like, lips poutin', like, cleavage heavin' – all the clichés a virgin wants and needs. Everythin' she asked me I just nodded or shook my head or gid her a one word answer. We spoke about Mick and me Mom and Dad. What year of school I was gonna be in.

"'Av ya sin Rambo yet? 'E's a strong lad, that Stallone, ay 'e? Are yo' strong, Tim?"

She sat me down on the sofa and knelt down in front of me. I arched my back and lifted my arse as she slipped my joggers off.

"Looks like yom ready already," she said.

An' I was, to be honest. I just nodded, like. I day speak to her. She straddled me an' slipped her knickers to one side as she sat down, easin' my cock into 'er.

"Just let Nicki tek care 'a ya, Bab."

14

You know what it's like, the first time like, well, maybe you do. You sorta imagine the feeling beforehand, like, but it ay the same. Honestly, I don't think anyone has that total bodily – pins an' needles – shiver – feelin' until you do it for the first time. It was warm an' wet an' I felt close an' safe ... but terrified too.

Honestly, I was a stallion. Nicki was impressed.

"Bloody 'ell, bab, this ay yer fust time is it?"

I nodded and smiled, like, an' she went quicker but nothin' was happenin'. She didn't give up though.

Honestly, after about an hour or so, I dunno, summat happened. Changed the mood, like. We were at it, an' she was grindin' an' all, an' we must 'a been in the zone 'cause we didn't hear Mick come in.

The door to the front room opened an' he stepped in, like, an' we didn't realise until he spoke.

"Sorry, Nic, I day realise yow 'ad company."

I tried to jump up, like, but Nicki 'ad me pinned, an' you remember, she was a big girl an' I wasn't exactly Chuck Norris. My heart went double-bump-stop - dum-dum, like. Mouth dry, like. Nicki waved her hand at him – like she would if she was busy makin' his tea an' he was pesterin' or summat. Just a sorta casual wave, like. An' Mick, he sat down on the arm on the chair opposite and watched it.

Honestly, he sat watchin' his wife fuckin' a teenager, arms folded like the news was on the telly. He sat watchin', an' I watched back. Watched his grubby, dry hands, his tight jeans, stained with three days travel,

15

his creased and stubbled face, his wide eyes, pale blue, staring at us. It wasn't a pervy look, like, an' it wasn't angry. It was the look of a man who was relaxed. Ya know, like the look on a man's face when he takes the first sip of his pint on a Fridee? So he has his first sip. He does it every week, so he knows what it's like – it's a knowable enjoyment like – that's the look he had. An' I looked back. An' she was still ridin'. An' thass when I felt it. Thass when I come ... It was strange.

Honestly, I'd come loads of times, as I said. I knew what to expect. But this blew me head off. It ran right up my spine and down to my toes, like, and I thought I might faint.

As soon as my dick stopped twitchin', Nicki got off, did up 'er robe, like, an' walked into the kitchen with a smile.

"Cheers, bab," 'er said. "Show 'im aart, Mick".

Mick put one hand on my back an' gid my shoulder a squeeze, like. Walked me to the door.

"Yo'm Carrick Carmody's lad, ay ya?"

I nodded an' walked off. I day say goodbye or thanks or nothin'. Honestly.

"See yo' soon, youngun."

And that was that, like.

Joyce

I still have nightmares. Most nights that Wych-Elm appears in my dreams. With its twisting, spindly, spider leg branches all coiled and curled into each

16

other, ferreting their way out of that hulk of trunk – all wet, brown, mossy. It loomed over the place. It looms over my dreams. I could be dreaming of all sorts of lovely things; big feasts, lottery wins, family parties, whatever, then it'll come. The Wych-Elm calls.

The dream breaks with the sight of those old fractured factories, the ruins and waste grounds of concrete, brick and rust, and then the tiny path that leads between the empty works and into Saltwells. It's a dream when you walk it now, really. You go from the little row of shops with neon lights – people putting the gas on their cards, buying their Friday chips, traffic passing outside – past the church and round through the terraces in Derby End. Then you face the grey and orange of the decayed metalwork machines, you cut through it and suddenly you're not in Netherton anymore, you're in the green and brown, the moist dirt of Saltwells. You trip up on nature. Nature trips you up.

Anon

I was in the Bull most nights. We all went for at least a couple.

We sid 'er a few times an' we day trust 'er. It was me what pointed it out to Alfred. Yo' spot a stranger a mile off round 'ere. Weem together. We look after each other. We goo to the sem church, the sem pub, the sem factory floor. Weem the sem. Weem together.

I wo say we enjoyed it. It 'ad to be done. But we was

17

proud, in a way. We was proud of each blow. Each time the burch came down on that 'arlots flesh.

2

Michelle

Who put Bella down the Wych-Elm?

I just found it mesmirisin'. Compelled to know.

Nicki was a middle-aged wench on the estate. 'Er was big, not ugly, but a big girl. 'Er always looked nice. She med a lot 'a what 'er 'ad. Always dressed in dead nice clobber an' the lads loved her tits. She day 'av kids, an' only worked part time at Sheena's shop, an' 'er fella, Mick, was a long haul lorry driver. In short, 'er'd *helped* quite a few 'a the lads on the Sledmere.

All the lads was like that. Obsessed. We'd 'a bin in the third year 'round that time an' all the lads 'ud be fiddlin' wid emselves, crackin' jokes that wor really jokes, mekkin' up stories. Yo' could always tell who was mekkin' it up. Tim wor like the rest of 'em.

"I was away at me cousin's in Solihull," Sam'd say. "Them posh down theya".

"It was Cath's birthdee," Jay'd copy. "An' 'er 'ad 'er mates over. It was Layla who 'ad 'er eye on me".

"Posh girls am sluts," another lad jumped in. "'Er gid me a blow job".

All the girls pretended to be sick. All the lads was fixated. It was always the sem. I lost my Vs on the weekend, one'd say. Yo' doh know 'er, 'er's from Leasowes, they'd say. An' sometimes our Tim'd overhear an' try an' get in on it. 'E day do well.

'E was always a bit odd, Tim. Strange lookin', an' all. The rest 'a Sledmere kids'd muck about down by the cut. We'd jump the water an' climb over the locks, an' we'd piss about in the ruins 'a Cobb's Engine 'ouse - which used to be where they'd pump water for the colliery but was now home to graffiti wars between Baggies and Wolves fans an' where we'd 'ave cheeky smokes. When we was doin' this though, Tim was down in the thin line 'a trees 'avin' a tug. Then 'e went to Nicki.

It wor too bad back then. We day know everyone, and they day know all of us, but bob a job, trick or treat, Christmas carols, there wor anythin' to werrit about kids gerrin' touched up or thieved back then. I doh know where Nicki stands on that, Tim was only fourteen then, I'm not sure she did anythin' all that bad really.

The dads all probably had a goo too.

I day know Tim too well back then, just sid 'im

about, acting strange. 'E looked strange an' all. Always wore black. 'Ad black hair, dyed black, back combed in a frizz. 'E was pale. Big brown eyes. You'd 'ear sounds like chainsaws comin' out 'a 'is 'eadphones. 'E was a quiet kid, kept to isself. But lookin' back 'e 'ad a look about 'im – like 'e day fit in but knew warr'e wanted. Like 'e was alright on 'is own, determined. This look in those deep brown eyes of 'is was the same when we met up all them years later. All them years later, you'd see summat in him as 'e spoke.

'E knew how to tell a tale, Tim did. 'E wor a liar but, well, me nan 'ud say 'e never let the truth gerrin the way of a good tale. But you cor be sure. I remember as a bab, I dropped a pet Guinea Pig an' it 'ad to be put down. I remember it in full-colour memory an' I felt really bad. I still do. I still 'ave all this guilt about it. But a few months back Nan'd said it wor never me, it was Grandad. Now Nan says 'er remembers it as well as I do so whose yed you gonna trust?

Nicki fucked 'im, like so many other lads. Normally they were older than Tim, they'd repay 'er for gerrin' us bottles 'a cider from Sheena's. Like I said, Tim was different, 'e day do things the sem as the other lads.

Tim gid me all the details. 'Ow 'er bit 'is collar bone an' pinned 'is wrists behind 'is back. 'Ow 'er lifted 'erself up and down lightly, 'ow 'er arched 'er back an' flicked 'er pelvis back an' forth. 'E said 'er was graceful an' dainty, well, for a big wench. 'An 'er talked to 'im all the way. An' 'e day say a word. 'E day even look at 'er, I doh think. I sorta wanted 'im a bit when 'e was tellin' me, odd as 'e was.

Now, when I was about fifteen me an' Sam did it on the Buffery Park – it was 'is fust time an' 'e day last long. An' a few wiks later me an' Jay did it too, when 'is folks was on nights, an' 'e day last long neither. Like I say, Tim day do things like the other lads. As 'e tells it, 'e lasted ages. It wor tharr'e day enjoy it, 'e just day come.

Tim told a tale an' 'e enjoyed tellin' it. I'd said to 'im I wor bothered if 'e liked boys or girls or what. It was 1995 an' 'e was a mon in 'is twenties now, an' 'e could mek 'is own choices. Only 'e liked to tell a tale, an' 'e'd said 'ow 'e knew about Bella an' the Wych-Elm.

Bella

Memory is difficult. I can barely piece it together. I can see the tree and I can sense the woods – all the filthy dusk of it. But memory is difficult. Memory is difficult when you're dead. There's no sense of self or space or time, just a sideshow of fragments. I can see the tree and I can sense the woods. There's lust and moisture, kisses and touches. Memory is difficult.

I can see the tree. It sits thick and squat. Dry skin warts over every inch of trunk and branch. Mosses creep in cracks of bark. I see brown, umber, khaki, tan. It is too heavy for itself. Too heavy for the soil, ripped, sucking at roots. Covens of fungi pitch plots about the base. Lovers' words etched in by penknife strokes – saps still spitting from the new tattoos. She wrote our names in there, but memory is difficult.

I can sense the woods – all the filthy dusk of it. Our tree sits thick and squat in barren mud, fenced off by a circle of brackens and beech. Back from here are barely visible paths, beaten down by footprints of us who needed seclusion. You cut through brambles, nettles, foxgloves that nest in dead bellpits. Currents of brown and green breed from clay-brine spas. She led me by the hand through here.

Memory is difficult when you're dead. It is the click-snap-rustle that ferrets in echo-claps through these woods. You don't see the birds and rodents but they're here. A newt plops, unseen. Adders coil under piles of wood limbs. They see you as you step away from others.

There is lust. She held my hand as we stepped to the tree. Rubs a thumb along my finger to reassure. Each step speeds the heart. She knows the way despite the dark. You still sense Saltwells' lush. She led me by the hand to that circle of bracken and beech. There is lust and moisture, kisses and touches. Here against the Wych-Elm.

This is where she led me. I see the tree and I sense these woods. I am still here. You call me Bella.

Michelle

As long as I remember there's bin a pub down Saltwells. At the visitor's centre, just before you gerr'in to the woods. Nan an' Granddad'd tek us down

23

sometimes. Me an' Gem loved to gerr'our food order ticket, wait for the number to be called out an' rush over to the counter to grab the tray. They used to be dead busy with dog walkers an' visitors but the woods am desolate now, the visitor's centre is padlocked and covered in weeds. So what weem left with is a massive old pub that only an 'andful 'a people use. There's a few of 'em around 'ere, enormous old places that only 'ouse the landlord an' a couple 'a regulars. Them black 'oles, Gem says. Now, I doh believe in ghosts an' witches an' that, but if you listen to the stories they'd tell you, iss haunted. Phil, who runs the Saltwells pub says 'e doh let 'is wife down the cellar.

"I cor tell you exactly," Phil said. "You just gerr'a feelin'. Like 'er's watchin' you. It ay nice. It builds on you. I goo down to sort the barrels out an' at fust you doh feel it, but iss like a pot 'a boilin' water. It sorta builds up around you. Imagine summat stalkin' you, not a person, like a cloud – it follows you and spreads around you as it closes in. Then it surrounds you. Then it starts to shrink around you. Thass wharr'iss like".

Phil called it a wench. 'E ant sin it but 'e knew it must be Bella.

It was great 'round 'ere as kids. We always 'ad somewhere away from parents to goo. There was always some bush or abandoned place to play in. Always summat to block the moms and dads out. We 'ad places where you could be in an enchanted forest, then the ruins of a castle. We could be in the fairy glen or rally drivin' in an abandoned escort. Then, we

24

always 'ad places to goo fer smokin', drinkin', kissin' lads. It was great. Ya knew where you was but yo'd be able to feel lost too. Ya wor more than a minute from 'ome, but nothin' was 'omely theya.

We wor aloud in Saltwells.

We knew we wor aloud in Saltwells on our own. They 'ad pits an' mires an' stuff that'd swalla' you up or brek ya neck slippin' down. Most 'a the time we stayed out, just day tell anyone when we did goo in. We'd 'eard about the Wych-Elm back then, everyone 'ad. But wid 'onny 'eard on it wi' silly kid stories. We day know the full story. It was haunted. Witches lived theya. Thass wheya *The Thing* comes from – we'd watched a tape 'a *The Thing* at a sleepover at Dawns an' it was the fust eighteen wid sin. We day sleep for a wik after.

Back when we was ten, Round Oak Steelworks 'ad just closed an' all the dads were on the dole. Some on 'em went scrappin', or tekin' slate or nickin' copper. Some on 'em become security guards, watchin' the slate an' copper. Some on 'em was nussin' pints in Ma Pardoes an' cussin' the racin' post. Warrever. They was around more them summers an' them day want us under theya feet.

Thass when we started gooin' down the cut more. It wor far from the estate but the thin strip 'a bushes and trees between acted as a border and shield for us. We became different down there, away from the eyes of adults. I remember Shahid. 'E was desperate to be in the gang and 'e'd do anythin'. Jay an' Sam were the bosses, they day say they was an' we day tell 'em they could be, they just was.

Sam'd say, "swim the cut from this bridge to that and y'am in, mate."

Shahid'd gerrin an' we'd watch 'im try an' swim, but 'e was poor an' ant bin to the baths an' day 'av no muscle on 'im so it was just like watchin' tadpoles stuck in a puddle, flippin' about an' wrestlin' for life. I 'ated tadpolin' – med me organs quiver. When 'e was a few meters up the cut Jay an' Sam 'ud turn around an' nod. We knew what the nod meant. All of us legged it up the tow path towards the Dudley Tunnel.

"Leave the Paki flounderin'."

I doh say Paki anymore but me Nan an' Grandad did 'cause they day understand 'ow Tom's Cobbler's 'ad become Sheena's shop an' they day lerr'um pay on a Fridee.

"You need bread now, Mr Langford, you bloody pay bread now," Sheena'd say.

Sheena was Shahid's mom an' 'er run a tight ship. 'Er day let more than three kids in at a time an' Shahid 'ad to be home at five. 'Is dad was a big bloke, you'd see 'im chasin' the skins down the Halesowen Road – ten 'a them, one 'ar'im.

Once, we'd dared Shahid to goo in Saltwells woods an' find the Wych-Elm. 'E was like 'is Dad, 'e wor scared 'a nothin' 'cept Sheena, so 'e went in, day 'e. It was summer, so at four there was loads 'a light left an' we promised to wait where the visitor's centre was, an' this time we meant it – we picked on 'im a bit but even Jay an' Sam knew that' the Wych-Elm was fuckin' scary, an'

26

non 'a us 'ud goo lookin'.

I doh know how long we waited. I ay sure if it was an hour or two or what, it was summer an' we was only ten, but we did know 'e should'a bin back be now an' it was gerrin' black over Bill's mother's, an' you could smell that steamy-fermenting smell that meant the sky'd crack soon. Jay an' Sam day want to but me and Gem said it was best so we all run 'ome. We went an' told Grandad and the bosses went to Sheena's to tell Mr Hussain.

"You stupid bloody kids, I bloody show you." E'd said.

"We'll both bloody show 'em when weem back, Sid, wo' we?" Grandad said. We day know why the dads called 'im Sid. I think it just helped 'em not to 'ate 'im.

Grandad knew where the Wych-Elm was, 'e said 'is mates went lookin' when they was kids. Grandad day tell anyone nothin' about 'is life. E'd tell us 'e served, tell us 'e lost 'is mom young, tell us 'e met Nan at the Grand in Wolves when 'er was sellin' ice-creams. Grandad day gi' ya nothin' else.

"We met at the Grand, remember Stan," Nan'd say.

"We did ar," was all the reply we 'ad.

"Shahid was sat at the trunk, slumped over, shiverin', wor 'e," Grandad day mince 'is words. "E day say a word all the way owm, 'e day. Non 'a you lot are te goo in te Saltwells again, yo' ay."

Grandad 'ad some cuts on his knuckles like where 'e'd wrestled against the 'awthorns. Mr Hussain 'ad a tear in 'is eye. 'E day stay to bloody show us, just

27

hurried Shahid home. There wor much that changed after that day but Shahid gorrin' the gang an' we day test 'im anymore, 'e never seemed that pleased about it. There wor much changed after that day but Grandad stopped werritin' about never gerrin' a tab at Sheena's, an 'e took Sid for a pint in Turner's on a Sundee every now an' then.

"Gerrin' the 'ouse," Grandad shouted. Thass when 'e told us about Bella.

'E never said much, Grandad day. 'E'd sin things. 'E'd done things. 'E was the sort you sid in the corner of the pub who day look much now but you still wouln't risk tekkin' on. There was three of 'em down the gulley one Sunday after Turner's. They asked Grandad for 'is wallet.

"Call an Ambulance," Grandad said. Then 'e swung three punches and sent 'em all out. 'E'd sin things. 'E'd done things. It was the fust time we'd properly heard about Bella. 'E day say a lot. We'd all 'eard Bella tales – it was the fust time an adult'd told us. The fust time it'd sunk in properly. 'E sat us down at the table an' Nan 'ad put out 'er banana bread. 'E gid us a look an' we knew 'e'd say it once an' we wor to interrupt.

"It ay just a story, our kid, it ay," Grandad started. "Iss theya, ay it? I doh know where 'er comes from or what 'er wants, I doh, but 'er's theya, 'er is. When me and your nan were courtin' we used to walk in Saltwells after tekkin' 'er mom to church, we did. Your nan day see it, 'er day. I rushed 'er off before 'er could. But I did, day I. I 'eard a noise, like a little scurrying sound,

I did. I was a bit of a baiter back then, wor I, so 'ad me catapult with me, I did, thought I'd 'eard a squirrel or summat so turned, day I. It 'appened too quickly to tell properly. 'Er body was pressed flat against a tree, it was. 'Er 'ead was turned towards us, wor it. 'Er 'ad wide, wild eyes, day 'er. I day know if 'er was shocked or angry or what. 'Er looked frozen, 'er did. 'Er looked scared. There was a yellow bit 'a fabric hangin' from 'er mouth. Thass 'ow I think it was, lookin' back, anyhow. I day stop to think at the time, I day. I grabbed your Nan and we legged it, day we, an' we ay never bin in since, we ay."

I doh believe in ghosts or witches an' that, an' I day believe properly back then either. But there was summat in Saltwells, an' there was summat about the Wych-Elm. I doh believe in ghosts or witches an' that but I reckon if summat 'appens somewhere it sorta leaves a dent or an echo in the place.

When Nan 'ad a barney at Grandad for missin' tay 'cause 'e'd bin down Pardoes . . .

"Bloody suppin' an' yappin' about Baggies and Wolves while ya beef dries out, we ay med 'a money, Stan"

. . . you could taste the feelin' of the argument afteruds even if you wor theya. Thass whar' I mean, a sort 'a dent in the area. Like walkin' down Lodge 'ill to Merry 'ill, the factories wor theya no more, an' iss all a massive glass an' plastic shoppin' centre now, but everyone from a square ten mile around 'ud feel the ghost 'a the steel mekkers an' you'd know it used to be

29

a big deal. Thass what Saltwells 'ad – the echo of summat big thar'appened.

Back at school Tim 'ad a couple 'a mates an' they used to just sit around swappin' stuff, an' they wor no good at footy, an' they wor no good on sports day, an' they day mix wi' the other lads. You'd see 'em down by the sports 'all, scribblin' Sisters of Mercy an' Bauhaus on theya pencil cases. Our Gem spotted 'ow Tim'd always be checkin' 'is nails, 'er'd spotted him gooin' to the bogs all the time, 'e was always scrubbin' 'is honds clean. There'd be a few times when we'd shout names at 'em, mebee nick 'is 'owmwork, but we day do nothin' too torturous an' Tim day bring it up them years later, an' 'e day seem to 'old a grudge wi' me any road.

'E wor on 'is own, it ay like we singled 'im out. There was 'im, Dave and Rich – always together. They did things. Played around with each other. Touched each other, like. I ay sure iss that odd really.

Gem was the girl I played around with. She lived wi' me, Nan and Grandad, I think 'er was Uncle Joe's kid, but I doh know an' 'e wor a proper Uncle.

"Why doh you pretend I'm Sam, an we can see who's the best kisser?"

We sid it as practice, really. I think loads 'a kids do it.

Like I say, we picked on Tim a bit an' 'e was odd but 'e 'ad Rich and Dave, an' 'e wor never put out by much. 'E was focused. Never phased. I said about Tim's eyes, day I? Even back then. Even though 'e seemed like 'e shoulda bin a shy kid who kept to 'isself, an' 'e did kip to 'isself, 'e wor shy. 'E was focused. Never phased. When 'e did summat, 'e did it 'cause 'e wanted to, an' you could tell just by the look of 'is eye.

Joyce

I've lived here nearly all my life. I grew up in Penn when the last bits of rationing were still happening. I got the job at this school when I was twenty-three and I was happy here, working hard, all the way into my seventies. It was more than work. My auntie and uncle were from Netherton so we used to come here quite a bit as kids, me and my cousin would sometimes go to Saltwells. We'd play games with some of the other kids on the estates, hide and seek, that sort of stuff. We never ventured too deep, we sort of wanted to but didn't want to either. There's something there and you know it's horrible but you've still got to have a sniff, still got to test it, still got to get close to it, ingest it somehow.

I knew Netherton pretty well, knew it all my life. When I got to around thirteen, fourteen I stopped mucking around with my cousin and her mates and started hanging around with some of the kids up on Cinder Bank, when we came to visit. I'd seen this girl called Yvonne, she had something about her.

We were playing hide and seek or something and one of the lads from the Cinder Bank gang shouted over.

"Am yo' the girl guides or what, yo' babbies."

"Shut your face," I shouted back, I was never put out by anyone. Never have been.

"Yeah, shut yower fairce, Eric," another voice said. Then she appeared. Came around the corner of the street and just leant against the wall. Leather jacket. Cigarette. Little grin. It was Yvonne.

"Alright, bab?"

She nodded her head for me to come over.

The Cinder Bank lot were all cool, I was used to the cousins. Yvonne had something else though. She had this giggle – a half cough, half squeak – it was cute. They were a couple of years older than me and they'd just started wearing leather and grease in their hair. They had Jackie Wilson and Little Richard LPs. My cousin was still singing Harry Belafonte songs.

We were no good, at least we tried to be no good, and we loved it. After a bit I used to catch the bus from Penn to Dudley and then walk down to Cinder Bank. Save me waiting for the next time we visited. Besides, when you're a teenager, if you miss a week with a group of mates you may as well just lock yourself in a room on your own and plan how many cats you're going to have when you grow up. I went to the girls' grammar school in Wolves so I hadn't had boys as mates before, and if the teachers caught any whiff of a Jerry Lee Lewis attitude then you'd get the cane across your hand, so down here I was someone else, someone who had a biker's jacket and boyfriends. I kept my jacket at Linda's, about three of us did. Linda's parents didn't care too much. We kept out of trouble,

32

in the main, and they were old freaks who'd spent the Twenties in Paris and Berlin.

Most of the time we didn't do much, just hung on the corner of streets or down by the factory gates flirting and smoking. Every now and then a couple would head off to the cemetery at Saint Andrew's or down to the reservoir.

I was from Penn and went to the girl's grammar school. The Cinder Bank gang were good guys and they didn't mention it much. Even when they did it was just curiosity. They weren't bothered if my mom and dad could afford meat each day, that he was a draughtsman and had a new car. They didn't care that I didn't have to share a toilet and we had a back garden. They didn't let it bother them, anyway. It seemed glaringly obvious to me. I was different and I'd end up different when we grew up, maybe they saw it too, they didn't let it bother them, that's all. All they were fussed about was that you didn't grass on anyone, you didn't screw any of us over, you bought your own cigarettes and you weren't a square. They'd talk about how they were doing woodwork when we were doing Latin, Linda used to make up names for the flowers and put on a posh voice:

"You see here, the dafodilous yellowus."

They'd ask about what it was like not having boys at school. Ernie and Eric used to joke about us all being inverts. We weren't. We definitely weren't.

Yvonne used to give him a look. Shut him up. She never said much.

Mom was a nurse at Walsall Manor, worked nights, so when I was back from school it was just me and Dad. Dad was great. He showed me how to do mechanical drawings and we went for walks in the park and he taught me about different trees and different birds. It was always me and him and he was great. He had a limp and smoked a pipe. You saw more people like that back then. People with limps and crutches and missing arms. We used to collect damsons and pears in Tettenhall, and he'd teach me how to pickle and dessicate. We had our own private scout group, I suppose, just the two of us. And I loved all that outdoors stuff and all those thrifty war gimmicks.

"Come on Joyce," he was always really excited, I was always catching up. "Come on. Come and see."

"I'm coming, Dad." He'd made it up the Sedgley Beacon, even with his gammy leg. "What have you got?" I came skipping behind.

"Honey Fungus, Joyce," his face was wild. You could see almost all of his teeth. His bushy eyebrows raised.

"Wow!"

He shook my hand and we ticked it off the list. He told me about the Funeral Bell that looked the same as honey fungus.

Tim

I 'ad Dave and Rich as muckers, to be honest. But I don't remember us bein' that close, it was a safety

34

in numbers thing like. We didn't like each other that much, but you've gotta have someone, ay ya?

Honestly, there was Dave, he sorta liked us more, I reckon. We had a sort of unspoken pact, like, that we'd look out for each other, an' we was all odd in our way, an' honestly, we all needed someone to watch our back an' pretend we were like everyone else. Dave was probably closest, but that was 'cause I knew how to get him to do stuff, like.

When he came 'round my house sometimes, when dad was out, like, we'd watch the sex scene in *The Terminator* an' I'd be the bloke an' he'd be Sarah Connor, we'd re-wind the tape an' then I'd be the wench. Honestly, we were only about nine so we didn't think anythin' of it really, we weren't naked an' we didn't actually do nothin', just rubbed against each other, like. Suppose that's what kids think being a grown up is. We still had girlfriends as we grew up, an' we didn't think anythin' about havin' boyfriends. Honestly, I didn't think on it 'til year eleven, at least. Maybe Dave did, he needed to be part of it more than me, like, an' Rich, I reckon. There was some kinda drive there, but I don't think it's any different to most kids, I honestly reckon most had a dally with a mate at some point.

Rich was the same, in a way, but we didn't do it as often, like, an' by the time we got to sixth we left him out, pretty much. Dave got into Bowie's *Tin Machine*, I had REM's *Green* on tape, and Rich started gooin' down 'is Dad's allotment. Me an' Dave started properly experimentin' then like, an' we had to keep that between us.

There were toilets in Netherton, underground ones, where the Anchor is now, like. That was too close to home for us. We'd heard about the toilets at Mary Stephen's Park in Oldswinford, an' we had to get the bus down – said we were going to the baths – missed the bus home an' walked up through the Delph. The Delph run was another spot, but the girls used that more than us, to be honest.

The toilets were tiny, stank of piss. No lights. Suffocating, dark green squares tiled every inch of it.

There was a language to it, like. A sort of way of gesturin', like. We got it wrong the first few times. If you spoke everyone'd leave. If you were too obvious everyone'd leave. You'd walk in an' you'd like, act normal – like you were havin' a piss, like. An older fella'd stand next to you, an' you'd see him look, an' you'd have to look, like but not look an' he'd lick his lips, an' then you'd get a suck. Honestly, you'd walk in an' you'd act normal, an' there'd be a bloke with his hands in his pockets, an' he'd be messin' with' 'is cock, but not really messin, an' you'd have to look but not look, an' maybe you'd do a quick gesture like, with your fist like, an' you'd end up havin' a two minute hand job in the cubicle.

We went a few times. Honestly, there was one bloke, much older than us. He got to know us a bit. Bryan. He was tall an' lanky an' gaunt but he 'ad lovely eyes an' a nervous, gentle way about 'im. Shaved head an' a bit of stubble, like, slightly grey. He must have been there half the time, at least. He'd only have to see me and Dave an' we didn't have to pretend to look but not look or do any gestures or nothin'. He'd lead us both into the cubicle. He was quick, he knew it had to be fast an' careful. He'd take off our trousers in one slick slide as he dropped to his knees. We'd be hard before he even started an' he'd swallow our cocks an' devour 'em. An' he'd always kiss us goodbye, honestly, he seemed to like that the most. He was lovely, to be honest, Bryan was.

But we didn't know what we were doin' an' we didn't know where to go. We just, like, knew we wanted to look for it. Dave didn't take any convincin'. See, back then we was doin' Blake in Sixth form, an' we had this teacher, Mr Crick, who proper loved Blake, like.

Dave wanted to pretend he was like the lads in *The Lost Boys*. I managed to get a summer of blow jobs persuadin' him cum was more a life-force than blood, so gays were modern vampires, like. He seemed to like it, an' I definitely did. He seemed to like to please me. We wor a couple, honestly, but even then we day see it as a gay thing. It was teenage experimentation, like. But more than that too – for us, it was Blakean, Shamanic. An' don't get me wrong, it was important an' we cared for each other.

Mr Crick taught us the War Poets when we'd finished with Blake. He never liked them as much and we started calling him Crick the Prick.

The first time I went all the way, like, was before all

this. Me an' Dave were sixteen. We took the day off an' Dave nicked his dad's whisky, an we went out to Saltwells. Dave had a book on paganism, like, he got from the library, an' in it, it said about how shamans used drugs and stuff to have visions.

Dave's brother, James – who was older than us by like three years – he'd said, "Yo' con boil up nutmeg for an hour an' drink it down, an' an hour later y'am trippin'."

Lookin' back we coulda and shoulda got some proper drugs but we day think it through an' part of us was too scared to go down the flats or the Wrenner. So we cooked up all his mom's nutmeg, it took her 'til christmas to realise it'd gone.

We swallowed it down, like. It was fuckin' rancid to be honest– a bitter, earthy, medicinal taste that burned your mouth off. Then we set off. I wanted to go to the Wych-Elm. Dave was scared, but 'e knew why we were there.

Honestly, I knew why we was there. We walked down by where the clay pits were, then struggled through the thicket to get away from the paths. We got ourselves to a little openin', like, where an old tree had collapsed, there was enough room for us to walk about in but it was enclosed by bramble an' bracken. The Wych-Elm was thick, dark – brittle-bark encased. Everythin' was flat, brown, shadowed around it. There was us an' the Wych-Elm, framed in this barren patch.

"Doh ate anythin' the night before," Dave'd said. "It acts as a sacrifice to the spirits, an' they'll see our intention an' then we'll 'ave visions."

After an hour the nutmeg hadn't done anythin', like, so we cracked into the Scotch. Dave had me dancin' around in a circle, like, an' we used tree stumps an' sticks for some tribal drummin', an' we did this over an' over, suppin' the Scotch as we went. It wor too long until we accidently collided as we danced an' I accidently landed on top of him when we fell.

Honestly, this was the fust time it'd bin tender. The fust time we'd properly kissed. There was romance to it, like, it wor just two lads, who couln't get a girl, muckin' about, it was proper sex.

An', honestly, it musta bin the fust time I'd sin Dave as a bloke I wanted to shag. Not just an exploit, like. I pinned his arms back and bit 'is collar. 'E'd rolled me over, spat on 'is cock an' fucked me. It was slow. Grindin'. Flesh gripped cock an' 'e eased in. Rockin'.

Gentle.

We lay on the ground in Saltwells, wrapped in each other's limbs, stinkina sweat an' cum an' shit an' the stale ferment of the wet woods, like.

To be honest, I'd love to know if he remembered it the same way. Tell him it was important.

3

Michelle

Gem, Nan, me – we all 'ad to deal wi' being talked down
to. I remember meetin' a lad from Guildford back when.
'E'd come down to slum it in Netherton one night, with
a chap 'e'd met at Birmingham Uni. Carrick was gerrin'
on at this point but 'e still gid 'im a kickin' for tekkin' the
piss on 'ow we spake. I remember lyin' in bed later that
night, thinkin' 'a all the witty things I coulda shurr'im
up with. *Esprit d'escalier* – the French call it. I'd 'a
told 'im that the way we spake 'is from the Germans an'
Vikings an' so it pre-dated 'is proper English, so 'e can
goo do one back to Surrey.

When we met up in our twenties an' 'e said 'e knew
about Bella, Tim'd always be lookin' up to check who
was listenin'. 'E'd check 'is nails – 'e still wore black
nail polish – then check who was in earshot. Burr'e wor

bothered who was. He wor never bothered if anyone gid 'im the eye. Non 'a our lot'd come down Stourbridge.

Tim was still really into Blake all these years on. 'E'd witter on about higher planes 'a consciousness an' comunin' wi' nature, an all that hippy bullshit them cranky, scruffy wannabes' use, to dress up theya selfishness. I've never met an hippy who did anythin' other. I remember a wench on holidee once, said 'er'd bin to Goa an' found 'erself, an' 'er was all righteous about Yoga an' macrobiotic an' everythin', an' 'er med a real point about 'ow we should all love each other an' step away from material wealth an' stuff.

Gem'd said, "Enlightenment's all well an' good but 'er day buy a round all night an' 'er smoked all that fat girl's fags, the bitch."

I knew a couple 'a wenches on the Delph Run, big dikes who'd knock anyone's yed off if you said anythin' or they sid you scowlin'. Gem worked with 'em at The Tenth Lock when 'er was eighteen, an' they 'elped us 'ome a couple 'a times when we'd gone past closin' time. We was different to them, an' Quarry Bank separated us, which meant a lot back then, but they was solid wenches who looked after ya.

"Gem's our Sister, an' yow am too, now."

I still sid Rich about. 'E still kept isself to isself. When 'e left school 'e gorra job at Corngreaves Golf Course. It wor a club, anyone could goo, you day 'ave to be a member or wear saft trousers. I think the kids round Halesowen and Colley Gate used it like we used the cut, more than anyone actually playin' golf. It was

42

another 'a them places in-between. One 'a them places 'a grass an' trees an' mud, just out 'a sight. Linking the flats an' 'ouses to the industrial estate. Rich cut the grass and looked after the place. 'E always loved nature an' that. 'E'd spend 'is wik tendin' the golf course, 'e's wikend tendin' 'e's allotment. It was 'is dad's, I think, but Rich liked it more. Now, when me an' Gem an' our lot am dancin' on the pool table an' linin' up shots, Rich is talkin' of vegetables.

"I cor stand petit pwars. Gi' me a marrowfat. Them the best ones, fuckin' king of the pays, the marrowfat."

Joyce

I started hanging out in Saltwells with Yvonne and the Cinder Bank gang. This was before all the graffiti and all the scary stories. There was something a *bit* scary about it, but that was woods at night; desolate, nothing to do with those rumours about witches and whatnot. The Bella story, later, was like the flu, it infected the whole area, morphed a little and got passed on. I don't think even the couple of dog walkers who pass it off as superstition can completely ignore it. Somewhere in their minds, Bella is there.

Back then, though, she didn't exist. We used to go down and muck about in the woods. We'd smoke and drink and kiss, throw stones at the windows of the factories, play hide and seek. Roundoak was on the edge of Saltwells back then, we used to break in and play in there too. I didn't like it too much but I liked the gang and didn't want to look like a wimp. It was Ernie who liked me, he'd always catch me and kiss me. I liked him too, but I wasn't ready to kiss boys. I did it though.

Yvonne was cool. She never said much, she just had a feeling about her. She was the only girl taller than me, had short blond hair – only boys had hair that short back then. Yvonne didn't care. She didn't smile at stuff really, you'd see her occasionally raise one eyebrow and purse her lips slightly. Her little cough-squeak. You knew then you'd impressed her. It wasn't a smile. It was a pout that showed off her dimples. She was lovely. Beautiful. Tough and cold, she never said much. I kind of hovered. Sometimes she'd roll her eyes at me when the others were being silly.

She was lovely. She lived with her parents and her little sister. We were her mates but she didn't have friends. Apparently, she hung out with the older boys at school. She had secrets. She never said much, I had to learn how to get her. Her uncle used to trade records in Liverpool so she had always heard the most recent LPs.

"Wass yower uncle got this wik, Yvonne?"

"A chap called Tennessee Ernie Ford, 'e said it was too close to 'ome for 'im an' summat I ay ever 'eard the like of."

Then she sang. "One for the money! Two for the show! Three to get ready now go, cat, go."

We never looked back.

There was something distant about her. She wasn't

44

spaced out or anything. She just sort of saw through all the nonsense and shrugged it off. Still, even when I didn't really know her well, I thought she had a little sadness in her. Some kind of muttering sadness that was trying to yelp. Maybe that's hindsight, though.

Tim

Me an' Dave lay there for a while, like, just daydreamin'. Listenin' to the sounds of birds an' squirrels fidget in the bushes, of the breeze, of seeds droppin' from trees. Layin' back and listenin' to the hum, whisper an' crack of the place. Then summat 'appened, like, changed the mood like. Honestly, I don't think either of us could say for sure what it was but it made us jump. It wor loud an' it wor bright – or dark – it was just a feelin', all of a sudden. I know this sounds saft like, but we both felt it an' we both said it felt the same. It was just a feelin' like.

Honestly, out of nowhere, at the same time, me an' Dave both thought someone 'ad sin us, someone was watchin'.

Michelle

I said I day believe in ghosts an' witches an' that but there was summat odd about Saltwells. I sorta felt touched by it.

I remember spillin' coffee on Nan's carpet once an' er'd just 'ad it new. I scrubbed it but it wor comin' up so I bought 'er a coffee table an' it covered the stain an' 'er thought I was the best granddaughter. Now that stain's still theya an' everytime I goo over to 'er house I can feel it, like iss whisperin' the secret – an' one 'a these days someone'll 'ear it.

I remember when we was about seventeen, wid started to goo to Turner's on a Satdee. Iss a scruffy pub between the flats an' the allotments. The sort with mud for a beer garden, frayed curtains, six dart boards in the back room which am never used. The wench theya wor bothered if we were under age an I doh think anyone outside 'a Netherton even knew where it was so no one was gonna call the police or anythin'. One night, Tim'd come in too. On 'is own.

"Dirty cunt," Sam'd said, an' a couple 'a the others joined in.

'E stayed for another pint, day look anyone in the eye, day respond to them, just sat, 'ad a couple 'a pints an' left. Sam an' three 'a the others saw 'im bein' quiet as an insult, like 'e was pretendin' they wor nothin' to 'im. They follo'd 'im 'ome.

They 'ad to wait til after school. Til we was almost grownups. Tim's dad was 'ard. 'E'd bin inside a couple 'a times. If you knew 'im an' 'e knew you, you was alright, an' if you gid 'im a nod an' quick *'ow do, Carrick?* but left it at that, then 'e was alright. Well, better than alright really, 'e 'ad ya back for life.

Even now Carrick's the sem. You'll see 'im walk into Turner's an' tek a quick glance around, like 'is checkin' who's theya an' where the exits am.

Grandad said, "thass what yo' was taught then, yo'

was, yo' goo in a place an' you check 'ow to gerr'out, yo' do, before you mek yourself at 'ome."

I think it was only Grandad who you'd see actually talkin' wi' Carrick, actually askin' an' answerin' like. 'E was 'ard, Carrick was. But, so Tim tells it, 'e wor all block'ead. As Tim says, Carrick still 'ad 'is mother's old recipes up on the wall in theya kitchen. It wor nothin' burr'a piece 'a paper with about six hand-scrawled instructions on it. But 'e kept it pinned on the wall.

"'Er day fuckin' need it," Carrick'd say. "'er was a bostin' cook. I think 'er 'ad it up 'cause 'er 'ad a saft fuckin' 'ead about jokes an' it med 'er loff."

When Carrick was in a good mood, an' not too drunk, 'e'd say 'ow 'e knew a wench called Una who was cousin to a bloke called Jack, who'd bin part 'a Bella's death. Carrick'd say 'ow Jack an' Una were drinkin' in Ma Pardoes one night. Some Dutch immigrant, an' a wench called Bella got drunk wi' 'em. Jack gid 'er a lift 'ome but 'er fell asleep in 'is car. Carrick day know why but apparently Jack an' the Dutchman took 'er into Saltwells an' stuck 'er in the Wych-Elm.

"Una said they was teachin' 'er a fuckin' lesson. They thought 'er'd fuckin' wake up in the cold 'a tree an' find 'er way 'ome, knowin' not to fuckin' drink wi' strangers again."

Jack ended up in a mental hospital, so Carrick says. "'E'd wek up in the middle 'a the fuckin' night – two eyes in the fuckin' dark, two fuckin' eyes spyin' from a tree trunk."

Tim

I wasn't picked on too much, honestly, think I had my dad's rep coverin' my back, like. Think they wanted to, like.

I don't see him anymore, I think he thinks I moved away.

To be honest, times were different then. Dad grew up when you had to be a fighter. It was like Sid an' Sheena an' Shahid these days, you stand up or get shit all over. Everyone was the same, they hated the Irish, an' even his teachers an' the police played their part too. Dad an' Uncle Tom'd go on about how they had to fight for everythin' 'cause the sign on every door said *No Blacks, No dogs, No Irish*, an' it was important that Irish came last, under dogs. They'd tell you stories . . .

"I stopped a couple 'a lads kickin' fuckin' shite outta 'a dog on the res one night, it ay fuckin' right that, so I stepped in. Gid the fuckers a good lampin' too. So the next day at school I got took in the 'ead teacher's an 'e lamped me back – said 'e knew it'd be a Paddy involved, day want to listen to wharrappened, just sid the name Carrick Carmody an' that was all 'e needed to know. Even the fuckin' police did the sem, they said "Y'am Pat Carmody's boy, ay ya", an' thass all they needed to know."

It wasn't like when the first immigrants came over, you know, like, they proper hated the Irish back then, an' didn't see nothin' wrong with lumpin' 'em at the bottom 'a the pile, like. They didn't have actual signs when Dad was growin' up, an' they didn't have actual laws to keep them down but they still had to fight, 'cause change doesn't happen just by sayin' the word, it trickles down, an' back on Lodge Hill an' the banks of Netherton it trickled down pretty slowly, like.

There were a couple of weeks in year nine or ten when Dave'd been off with mumps an' Rich was doin' summat else, so I was on my own, like. That's when I started up on the wankin'. I mean, I'd done it before, but, honestly, this is when it started in a weird way. So, one day I got stopped by Miss Wyatt.

She stopped me an' took me to her office.

She had to try an' be special, like. She never needed her own office, she was just a teacher. Her office was like a dentist's. It stank of cleanin' an' nothin' was out of place. She got me with the deep, Spanish Inquisition shit.

"Mr Carmody. I've seen you coming in and out of the toilets quite a lot today."

My heart sank, I had that empty stomach feelin' you get, like.

"Do you have a problem, Mr Carmody?" she said.

I shook my head and stuck my eyes to the floor.

"As you know, there are certain responsibilities and duties of care that are required of a person in my position, yes?"

"Yes," I said.

"So, if I see unusual behaviour, I'm compelled to act in some way that will protect the reputation of the school and the safety of its pupils, yes?"

49

"Yes Miss."

"I'll need you to empty your bag then please, Mr Carmody."

I kicked off, you know.

"Why?" I said. "What for? I wor doin' nothin'."

"Empty it or I'll empty it in the next assembly."

I cried. I wasn't scarred or nothin', like, but I was embarrassed an' when you're fourteen, fifteen, you're still a kid really, like, an' you cor just turn off that feelin' of havin' to cry.

"Empty your bag, please. Last time."

So I did, an' she found a porno.

I unpacked my bag an' there it was. Honestly, on her desk with my lunch box, pencil case an' books – a big, thick, glossy porno. Wyatt was quiet. She just looked at it for a few seconds, then picked it up. She held it with thumb and finger like it was diseased, an' she dropped it in her bin.

For a few more seconds she looked confused, like she didn't know what to say an' do next but she shook it off quickly an' got back to her hard self.

"I'll have to talk to Mr Price about this, Tim."

I started to cry again. Felt like I was gonna piss myself, like. If it got as far as Mr Price it'd probably get home, too.

"Doh tell me Dad, Miss Wyatt!" I begged 'er.

She knew. She changed again then, she was hard still but she sorta looked like she enjoyed it all. She had a look about her, like she was excited by it all – wide eyes, a tight grin in the corner of her mouth.

Other thing is like, it wor just a porno, it was like a scrapbook I'd med to be honest. I'd cut up loadsa different pictures an' put 'em back together. Mixed 'em all up, like, so they wor just the normal shots of naked girls looking confused at the camera. Mixed 'em all up so they wor just shots of 'ard men screwin' women. Med it me own, like. Med a cut up collage of all sorts of figures, they wor men and they wor women.

To be honest, Mr Price an' Miss Wyatt must've had a chat, an' I bet my dad's name came up 'cause they didn't call home. I had a week of detentions and told my folks I'd had a fight. Dad seemed pleased, like, but he still made me wash his car an' clean the tops for mom.

"Thass 'ow it works, our kid. Yo' pay yo' fuckin' dues, even if y'am in the right."

Any road, this is why the lads hated me, an' this is why they followed me home after Turner's, like. See Wyatt hadn't done the right thing, she didn't not tell my dad 'cause she knew what he was like, she just didn't want to have to have him up at the school, like. They didn't want to have to worry about Carrick Carmody so she dealt with it herself. Honestly, 'er turned the school against me.

Dave

"Let's go to the Wych-Elm," 'E'd said. *I day want to. E 'ad ways 'a persuadin' me. Like that time I sucked 'im off. 'E 'ad ways, the cunt.* My fuckin' jaw is killin'. An'

these sores. I'm shiverin' but I'm 'ot, too. This blanket needs changin'. Gotta get some soup an' some 'a them cold and flu drinks. I'm gonna need to blaze in a bit. I'll goo see Tomo an' pick up some spice. Pick it up with left-over crank.

We were dancin' in the woods. I doh think Tim took it serious. Skippin' an' spinnin' an' stompin' our feet. We went 'round an' 'round. The woods were odd. They always was. They were always talkin' about Bella. Even on a sunny day them woods were damp – 'ad that resin smell. I could go for some resin. You cor gerrit now. Wid goo down the Parkhead Viaduct an' you'd bong it from the cut. It was only down the road from the estate but we were out 'a sight. By bushes an' birds an' rodents an' buttercups. Spend an' hour just loffin'.

I need a doctor. These sores, them blisterin'. *We 'ad nutmeg that day, it day work for me but Tim sid summat that day. They say that about nutmeg. You'm better off on predictable drugs. It was slow motion when 'e came at me. We was dancin'. Thought we was comunin' wi' nature – I'd looked at books on white witches an' the red dog saloon. It was spring an' the bluebells were out – pokin' up in patches through bracken. The spunk smell 'a pollen an' soil.* See, I cor stop itichin' an' when I itch iss cuttin' me up an' them weepin' – I'm off to Tomo's as soon as the sun comes up. *It was slow motion when 'e came at me. Like 'is big brown eyes was swallowin' me. See Tim 'ad these eyes, just big, intense dark. 'E was lovely. No one else sid it back then. The bastard, 'e soon changed.* If I just get up, 'ave a quick smoke with Tomo, sort through last night's crank an' then I'll get myself sorted – I need a new blanket – an' I'll get the cups washed an' I'll goo to the drop in an' see about these blisters an' tell the nurse about the shivers, then maybe I can look at gerrin back to Mom's. *I swear I 'eard the jackdaws an' magpies clappin' along as they fluttered. It was dark green an' brown an' the bits 'a light an' purple flower 'eads all spun together. 'E med it look like it was an accident, like 'e wor lookin', but the way 'e fell into me was sorta soft, 'e knew I was little, an' we both fell to the ground. I looked up. 'E looked back, them big, brown eyes wide. Tiny little dimples on the side 'a his smile. It wor more than a few seconds but it was longer, you know, longer in the yed, then 'e kissed me. We both knew it was comin' to this.* Me fuckin' jaw, an' these shivers, I cor think proper, my neck, just around my jaw, iss all swollen. *'E kissed me 'ard, tongue soft, ticklin'. 'Is 'ond stroked down from my neck, chest, hip. Slipped into trousers, grabbed cock. It was slow for a few seconds but I was 'ard in no time an' 'e started grippin' it an' 'e was like a piston. We kissed. 'Is lips pushed deep into mine. Our tongues searchin' our mouths.* I cor stop itchin, there's sores an' blisters an' rashes an' I cor 'elp it but them gerrin wuss. I 'ad the shits yesterdee. I ay 'ad nothin' to ate. *It wor long till I 'ad my 'ond on his fly, ripped down 'is trousers. I must 'a got some strength from somewhere – I turned him over an' 'is jeans come down an' 'e was on 'is knees, back arched, elbows, forearms, fingers, grippin the earth. 'E rooted to the dirt.*

53

I spat on me 'ond an' rubbed it on me cock an' I spat on 'is arse an' I fucked 'im. It was tough for a second. 'Is skin tightened around the end 'a my cock an' I pulled back. Waited. 'E breathed out. Deep. I thrust. Slow. Gently swayin' my hips. Gently pullin' in an' out. 'E stroked my thigh, reachin' back. I stroked 'is neck, cheek. Gently swayin'. Gently pullin' in an' out. Deep. Waited. Push. Wait. Pull back. Arched back. Rim tight an' twitchin. I've got the twitches. I need to goo see Tomo. Iss almost mornin'. 'E'll be up soon. Fuck! These blisters. I ay well.

We lay lookin' up at the soft sun an' the jagged branches. Black vines against the bright an' pale. Sweaty an' sticky with the muck 'a Saltwells on our flesh. I lay on 'is chest an' we cuddled an' 'e kissed my fore'ead.

'E flinched. Then I did. We wor sure what it was. I shook it off as a daydream. Tim said we 'ad to leave.

"Is someone theya!?" 'E 'alf asked.

I went back years later. Our names were joined in the bark 'a the tree. In theya, weem part 'a the echo 'a them woods.

4

Michelle

Miss Wyatt'd 'av ya back after school for not tuckin' ya shirt in, or laughin' too loud at lunch. 'Er day care about 'avin a punishment to fit the crime. If you was runnin' late an' 'er caught you runnin', you'd 'av the sem shit as someone who'd bin fightin'. There was only good an' bad with Wyatt. Right an' wrong. There wor degrees of it. 'Er was a weird wench. Old – too old to still be workin'. Big too. 'Er was big as a bonk oss, too big for a wench really. 'Er 'ad a funny way about 'er. There wor no room for rule bendin', or turnin' blind eyes. 'Er was always tightly wrapped in 'er clothes an' 'er clothes were always crisp.

'Er 'ad a separate office. 'Er wor nothin' 'cept a normal teacher, but 'er 'ad to 'ave 'er own special office. Everythin' was always in iss place, always surgical.

I s'pose we all like stuff in iss place, doh we? It ay like we cor gerron an' what not, iss just that we like stuff in iss place. Maybe we see ourselves better by seein' what's different. There was more to it for Wyatt, 'er relied on it, 'er day function without divides.

Shahid was our mate, 'e was the sem as us in loads 'a ways, but sometimes 'e stank 'a cumin an' talked to girls in funny ways. Thass enough difference, an' difference we were used to. Tim wor our mate, but we day gi' 'im an 'ard time until the rumours started up. We knew 'e was different an' sometimes we took the piss a bit, but it wor really a big thing. Wyatt marked 'im out as proper different.

Imagine it. The toughest teacher in school, an' the sort who probably 'ad a seal on 'er minge 'cause 'er was savin' 'erself for Cliff Richard, an 'er 'ad a shrine to 'im too, probably. Miss Wyatt was tough, she day tek no prisoners, day suffer no fools, an' 'er day care for any 'a that sort 'a stuff.

Nan'd bin to school wi' 'er, back when they was kids. Nan went to the Girl's Grammar School in Wolves, 'er was smart, Nan was, read every day. 'Er'd never gerra question wrong on Blockbusters, said 'er wanted to be a spy when 'er was a kid, but 'er met Grandad an' me dad was born.

"'Er was med 'a steel back then, that Wyatt wench, 'er was, 'er' was ar," Nan said. "'Er was 'ead of the choir, 'er was', an' captain of the 'ockey team, ar, 'er was popular, taller than the rest on us, not a tart but 'er knew 'ow to play the game, 'er did, ar. It wor a rough school, it wor, so there wor much fisty-cuffs, but if you crossed Joyce Wyatt, 'er'd turn the school against ya, 'er would ar. 'Appened to my mucker, Diane, it did, 'er ad to leave after a to-do on the 'ockey pitch one lunch time, 'er did, ar. Wonder warr'ers up to now, Diane Bennett?"

Nan'd tell me an' Gem a different story about Bella.

"'Er was a gypsy wench, 'er was. Sold 'er soul to the devil so 'er could 'av power over life an' death, 'er did, ar. But the devil's a trickster, ay 'e, an 'e day tell 'er she'd be locked up in the Wych-Elm an' er'd only be able to use 'er power each 'allows eve, ay it."

Then Nan'd jump up an' shriek, an' me and Gem u'd run around the front room. Nan loved that stuff. Me an' Gem still tek 'er up to see the horror films at the pictures.

No one knew the truth about them rumours an' Tim. They come outta nowhere really. No one questioned it. *Yo' 'eard about Brolley?* No one was told what'd actually 'appened, but one way or another, it'd gorr'out that Tim Carmody was a perv.

Flashed at a mom an' 'er kids, day 'e?

Mr Price sid 'im playin' wi' isself with 'is tie wrapped about his neck.

I 'eard 'e was watchin' people shit in the loo.

I reckon the story changed every few months an' it'd depend who you was talkin' to but for the last couple 'a years 'a school we all behaved like Tim'd done summat really vile, an' even though he wor non 'a our mates, we all acted like 'e'd disgraced us, like 'e'd lied, like 'e was a traitor. For some on 'em that disgrace outweighed their fear 'a Carrick.

Iss odd 'ow it 'appens. Like a virus or summat, it spreads. Some on us'd ask a few questions about it, try an' look like we wor being judgemental. But thass the power of it. Like Bella. Like nature tekkin' back control. We can shrug but, we doh never totally shrug it off. Wyatt'd spread them rumours, med 'im sorta criminal an' med 'im sorta contagious – an' we all bought it.

Tim, Dave an' Rich were always together, so we lumped 'em all in the sem way. To us they was all pervs. The rumours fucked 'em all. They stuck together though. Never left each other's side. An' if someone 'ad a truck with Dave or Rich, Tim day worry about standin' up an' that soon cooled 'em down. Iss Carrick's son. They were freaks, to be fair. They wore black an' liked The Cure, I like the Cure but they liked the borin' bits with no words too. Nothin' awful ever 'appened. I think Dave got spat on once and they'd always get roughed up a bit in PE, but that was sport, wor it? Mostly we left 'em alone. I remember some people sayin', you doh wanna get too close to 'em, like they'd pass it on. Silly really but it stuck. Even the teachers felt it I think. The way they handed out books. Who they chose to read. The grades they gave. It was better for them that the three freaks were invisible. Better if they day stand out or they'd infect the rest of us.

There was two science teachers we 'ad, an' everyone knew they was 'avin' an affair. I 'eard 'em once ...

"How do they expect to get on in life anyway?" one said, and he used words like human interaction an' social engagement an' all that.

"You're awful, Simon," the other said. (It was always a bonus learnin' your teachers fust name.)

"It's true though isn't it?" 'e said. An' they said ow they thought Tim an' 'is mates were gays, an' 'ow there was summat that'd fester an' infest, or summat.

"I think he's probably a homosexual, Simon," the one said.

"It's more than that from what Joyce told us and you know it."

Those two teachers always smoked at the back 'a the staff room. We 'ad a spot just on the other side 'a the gulley. The birr'a land that sits between the school and the park. There was a steep bonk an' then a flat patch 'a weeds an' dirt. They day 'ave a clue of all the stuff we over'eard 'em sayin'.

———————

It wor until we was seventeen an' gooin' down Turner's that anyone did anythin' about it. Years 'a pent up wonder an' anger, a few too many pints, bein' in a gang – just one face in a gang, the stupid, boyish confidence 'a young men – it all come together that night when they followed 'im 'ome.

They followed 'im 'ome from Turner's. Six on 'em. The quickest road back was to cut through the allotments, slip up the gulley an' into the estate. Thass the way 'e went an' thass the way we all went. At the end 'a the allotments ya meet a track. It ay a path, iss a birr'a land where the grass doh grow no more 'cause thass 'ow we all gorr'ome. So the track dips an' then rises an' thass where you meet the gulley. Thass where they gorr'im – at the bottom 'a the dip.

Some on 'em called it the rec, but it wor a rec, it was a patch 'a land that was always brown an' muddy, almost a perfect square 'a land that sat between the flats, all grey an' dusty, an' the redbrick terraces of Sledmere. 'E says 'e day 'ear 'em but 'e must 'av. Thing is with this sorta thing is you doh know if y'am being followed or iss just that them walkin' the sem way, an' if you do run, an' they ay stalkin' ya, then you've just med an enemy by thinkin' it. We all 'ad that from time to time. It happened to our Gem too. She 'ad a massive row wi' a wench called Kim once. Kim'd bin following Gem but Gem day know it was 'er. 'Er got shaken up an' legged it. Kim thought 'er'd dissed 'er an' it took us ages to convince 'er it wor personal.

Thass where they gorr'im. At the bottom of the dip. They talked about it in Turners for ages, showin' off about 'ow quickly 'is nose 'ad broken, 'ow you could see the bruises risin' from 'is kidneys. 'E took a proper beltin'.

Tim

Honestly, they caught up with me an' they kicked me feet away. They stood around an' they all started stickin' the boot in, like. All I could do was curl up an'

60

try an' cover me 'ead. I took a proper lampin', like. One lad 'ad a grip on me ankles an' was kickin' at me knees. Just stampin' an' kickin' at me knee cap, over an' over. One lad was puttin' the boot in around me stomach an' sides. One lad just 'eld me face, like, an' kept poundin' fists into it. I tried to wriggle an' hide the soft bits, like, but these guys were too many. They just kept beatin'.

Honestly, time slowed right down. I could see each clout slowly comin' but there was nothin' I could do

When me an' Dave fust 'ad sex in Saltwells, I could feel every second like a thousand, every thrust and touch like I was just one massive sensor, like. Time, space and senses do summat strange when summat important 'appens, like, they make you take it in an 'undredfold.

I knew they all laughed about what they did to me at the bottom of the dip. To be honest, they don't tell the full story though, I bet.

I was on the floor, takin' a kickin', like, an I'm practically unconscious, I mean they really took it out on me. Then, summat happens, changes the mood like.

"Gerr'outta it you bunch 'a bastards. I doh care what ya think 'e's done. I'll rip ya yeds off ya shoulders."

So, like, they all stop, like, an' they turn, an' they see Mick wi' a cricket bat, leggin' it towards them. An' then they leg it, an' leave me battered on the floor. Honestly, Mick picks me up, cradles me, an' he carries me back to him an' Nicki's house.

Honestly, my lip was split, my nose was screwed an' I had bruises all over my body. Nicki gave me a clean-up, like, an' she had some cream she said she got from Corfu that worked dead good on bruises. I asked Mick about why he stepped in, like, 'cause I wasn't sure why he wasn't afraid, 'cause if they'd turned on him he coulda got a kickin' too.

"We've gorr'a look out for each other, ay we? There ay many on us about."

He carried me upstairs. He was a big lad, like. He clutched me. He undressed me and placed me down in the bath. I stayed with them for two days an' that's when I thought I wouldn't go back home, an' honestly, I didn't.

Carrick

'E's my fuckin' son, ay 'e? But if 'e's a fuckin' faggot I doh want 'im under my roof. I've 'eard the shit they was sayin' down Turners. 'E's my fuckin' son ay 'e – I 'eard what they did to 'im an' they'll 'ave it comin' to 'em. I'll 'ave a word wi' Stan an' see wass true fust. Then skulls'll be fuckin' split.

I know warr' I'm like. I ay fuckin' clueless. I see wass 'appenin with all on 'em an' meself. I get like this when I've bin on me own too long an' I gerr'on the Jack. Fuck knows what our mom'd think of it. 'Er'd 'a took me up to ... no, fuck it. I'd 'a never crossed 'em like 'e as. 'Er was solid. Everyone fuckin' loved mom. Look at this, 'er 'ad a saft sense 'a humour an' 'er knew 'ow to kip an 'ouse gooin'. Yo' 'ad tay time round the table then. Everyone did. Look at this – thass 'er old recipe sheet.

Ivy's Fittle:
Groarty Dick
Soak your groarts the night before – one cup on them will do. Cut up an onion and a Leek. Chop your meat – cheek, belly or shin. Or just have the groarts, it doh matter. Stick it all in a stewing pot. Pop it in oven for a day.

Tongue
Tek your tongues from out the pickle. Give them a soak and sift off the muck. Boil them up for the morning with a few cloves and some cuts. Kip the boiling licka for broths.

Gray Pays and Bacon
Soak your pays in water overnight - a cup on them will do. Boil them up for a day. Cut your bacon and fry it in your lard (not butter, you doh have butter with bacon). Add the bacon and the licka to the pays.

I'll jump in the fuckin' cut, I ay bothered. No one wants me around now anyroad. There ay room now for an old steelman, an' an old Catholic. Iss fuckin' Irish in these veins. I cor blame 'em if them right about 'im bein' a queer, I'd 'a gid 'im a fuckin' kickin an' all. I know, I've bin on the Jack an' our wench is on nights.

Burr'is our kid too, our Tim. Fuck! 'E's lost to us now, ay 'e? I'll jump in the fuckin' cut. Yo' wait. Watch the central news in the mornin'. My mom, rest 'er soul, 'er warned me about it. Said 'e was on 'is own a lot. Said 'e was watchin' them vampire films a lot.

"Whataboutya, Carrick." 'er'd say. "Keep a savage eye on him, Carrick, it's unnatural. Fierce. Would you look at his hair?"

Ivy's Fittle:
Spring Pluck
Get a lamb's pluck and boil it. Kip the boiling licka for broths. Cut the pluck up handsome. Fry it up with lard (or butter on a Sunday). Add some of your larder licka.

Pettitoes
Get your pigs feet, heart and liver and boil them. After about 10 minutes tek the heart and liver out and mince them small. Stick them back in. Add flour and some lard (or butter on a Sunday) to thick it up. Have it with fried onion and bread. Kip your stewing licka for broths.

Cow Heel
Boil your cow heel and cut it up handsome. Dip the bits in egg and breadcrumbs. Fry them. Kip your stewing licka for broths.

Nah, it'll be them that fuckin' gerr'it. Mom was solid burr 'er'd tell yo' too. No one teks down a Carmody. No fucker. An' I know, I've bin on the Jack all night, ay I? But them lads berra fuckin' watch it. That Mick better watch it - 'e knows summat. I tell ya. I've teken bigger men an' more on 'em an' all.

Bella

It's hard to be clear when you're dead. Nothing holds in the same way. It's hard. I recall the smell of pig shit and how it slugs at my throat. When I lived I could get that smell in a mood. When the mood was right, I could smell it and every organ in me would flex and shiver. When there was a bad mood. That rank stench and body quiver – I'll never know where it came from or how it mustered so much feeling. That's what it's like now. My life is held in rushes of smells and the moods that flood with each sniff. Memory is difficult when you're dead.

Mom married Dad when I was still inside her. He worked days and she worked nights, so it was me and Nan. Me and Nan pulled potatoes in the field. She made the best chips around. Potatoes and pig shit. Sweat and soil. You would gag on it, and like the gag too, sometimes. I learned to like Dad's belt too, sometimes. Mom normally liked it for me. There's no pain out here in the woods. Just the spasms of smelling things. Memory is difficult and these spasms are like tears – they soothe and soil.

Dad had one leg. They cut it off in the trench. That cut saved the rest of him. He screams sometimes, he can still feel it. That's what you do too. When you wander in to Saltwells looking for the Wych-Elm, chasing rumours and that empty stomach feeling, you find the bit they cut

65

away. You call me Bella.

Memory is difficult but I see like cut crystal. I see you when you wander in. That brown skinned boy, he is terrified. Skinny limbs shivering. Sweat pearled over flesh. Deep brown eyes bold and wide. He breathes in gasps through a wide mouth. I don't know if he saw me but he froze. He froze at the Wych-Elm. Just stared. Stared straight through me. He was stiff. Then he collapses – slumped at the trunk. I stood and looked over him. I took in every pore of him. Then those older guys came and grabbed him and pulled him away. The oldest was strong. The oldest seemed to know more. He could see something of me. He said, Doh look, doh look at 'er. They carried him away in a rush.

Joyce

I was never a part of their gang really. Just kind of loomed about. I wanted to be with Yvonne. I wanted to be just like her. That meant leaning against the fence and having a fag, rolling your eyes at the ones that were still 'playing'. I had to learn how to get her but I was a fast learner. That's the way of it. That's how I was at school, that's how I carried on being. All I had to do was pick out the bits she wanted to keep in Eric and the others and get rid of the rest. All I had to do was kind of method act. It took a few weeks. No real hardship.

I'd taken some of Dad's cigarettes. I gave her a Camel.

"Y'am alright, yow am, Joyce," She said. "D'ya fancy

gooin' to the outdoor at The Bull. My old mon always sends us with a bob for 'is Mild so they know me."

I nodded and followed and tried to shrug and be with it.

"Iss onny down rode theya. We can come back 'ere an' 'ave a sup. Saves us pitherin' about with this lot."

Off we went, through the patchwork of red bricks to The Bull. I stood on the corner and Yvonne went to the latch to pick up a jug.

Some drunk passed by, saying what yo' doin' theya on the corner? Yo' look like yo'm workin' under the clock. I had no idea what he meant then.

The Cinder Bank lot were different. Yvonne was different again. I'd given her a Camel and done my best to be cool.

"Yo' doh say much, Joyce, ay? Thass cool."

Back at the church we drank the Mild. Yvonne swigged at it and I tried, too. She was lovely. Tall, blonde, hair short-trimmed around her face. She was pale, skinny – blue eyes that would splinter you.

"Wass it like at a wenches school? I know them all tek the piss but really, wass it like?"

"It's okay, as good as school can be."

"I know, ar. Ours is alright. I cor wait to gerr'out though. I ay like them. Warram the other wenches like?"

"I'm not like them either. Most of them had a bob on them," I said. "Faces like a fourpenny hock." She laughed her head off at that. Smiled at me. I'd heard

67

my auntie say it about mom. You'd freeze in Yvonne's smile. She was lovely. We weren't like them.

We became untouchable. Whenever we had anything to say we whispered it. It was cool. You really had to listen to hear what we said. That was never much, though, we said more with a raised eyebrow and an exhale of smoke than with sentences. We were cool and it was just me and her.

Even all those years later I wanted to be untouchable. All those years later I was still outside of it all. It had happened a few times at school. A few times growing up and as a teacher. Something got stuck in me when I was faced with that stuff. You know, sex stuff. Something needed addressing. I'm sorry. Something needed rebalance. And it needed to be kept away from me.

Yvonne

I was always bored. Mom and Dad never bothered so I never bothered with them. Eric and Ernie were dickheads an' the others was just kids. I 'ad to look after our bab most afternoons. I cor remember 'ow Joyce joined in. 'Er was different an' I sid straight off 'ow 'er looked at me. 'Er 'ad nice shoes an' a way 'a spaykin'. I lerr'er in.

"Y'am alright, yo' am, Joyce," I said. Yo' shoulda sid 'er face. 'Er went red in the cheeks, 'er did. 'Er wanted summat different too. I started tellin' 'er about Johnny Cash an' me plans fer life in America.

68

"I would just love that," 'Er said. 'Er gid me 'er fags, 'er could never smoke 'em proper anyroad.

'Er 'ad a look about 'er, Joyce did. 'Er was unsure. 'Er'd never bin down Saltwells. Never bin to the Outdoor or 'ad a drink. Every now an' then 'er tried to be like us, tried to spake it, like. 'Er liked skippin' an' 'er knew stuff about plants. 'Er 'ad a paleness about 'er. I was gonna colour 'er.

I sid at school 'ow standin' off a bit worked. Med people a bit worried, a bit protective, a bit more willin'. Joyce was the sem. Them all the sem. They'd do stuff. Anything. I'd sid it with Phyllis Dietrichson at the pictures when er says to the insurance bloke there's a speed limit in this state, Mr Neff. Yo' ay even gotta promise 'em nothin'. The fust time I gid 'er a hug 'er cheeks went red too – 'er cowered a little. I walked home wi' me shoulders back. 'Er cousin 'ad said they was poshos. 'Er dad 'ad a car. It only took *Yes Mrs Wyatt* and *thanks Mr Wyatt* a few times. Charm. It only took me a little smile, the odd hug – 'er was charmed. 'Er got me an LP from Bilston Market one time.

They took me swimmin', let me use 'er mom's bike. 'Er was in my palm.

5

Michelle

Our last year in sixth form was Miss Wyatt's last year too, but 'er should'a retired before, 'er should. She was old. Older than all of 'em. All teachers am old when y'am thar'age but Wyatt was dead old, I mean 'er coulda bin found on a dig at Dudley Castle. 'Er looked sorta like a skeleton, too.

Tim'd grown up quite 'ard, like 'is Dad. 'E was sorta gaunt lookin' but all muscle an' sinew. 'E'd 'a knocked 'er 'ed off 'er shoulders if 'e'd 'a caught 'er.

Wyatt was a fossil. 'Er was in a perfect place, 'round 'ere. We built all this on fossils. Underneath the council houses. Buried under Hingley's factory. Deep down beneath the tarmac, the foundations, the brick an' ores. Fossils. The bloody coat of arms is a bloody trilobite, ay it. See, the earth under all this modern

71

stuff is hundreds 'a millions 'a years old. Weem built on the clay and the lime that used to be home to reefs an' full 'a giant insects. It was pure survival back then. Fuck an' eat your way through life – it doh matter who or what. All these bugs got caught up in the claggy minerals and dried out. Iss all over. Iss all over the place. It gets into the water. It sits just below. Iss the roots 'a us. Iss where we all goo back to.

Tim'd lost some 'a the blackness now we was older. 'E'd bin away so e'd lost the coke in 'is voice an' all. 'E day look as pale. 'E was still odd. Still odd lookin'. 'Is cheek bones looked like they'd pierce 'is skin. 'Is eyes were sunken – deep brown. 'E was always fidgettin', checkin' 'is honds, iverrin' about to see who was lookin'. 'E'd start talkin', an' you'd see 'is eyes twitchin'. 'E wor nervous. Never sure who 'e was lookin' for.

Tim

I wor scared, like. But I 'ad to get away, even if it was just to the Lye, so I could properly be myself. Far enough away so it was safe to come out. Close enough so that I could look back too. Somewhere between safe and unsafe, like.

After I got the kickin', an' after stayin' with Mick an' Nicki, I didn't go back home. Mick said he had two weeks off work, like, so I could kip down there while they were in Malaga. An' when they were back, if I hadn't sorted anythin' out, then he had an old lorry cabin down the industrial estate near the Lye.

72

"Iss the sort we use on long hauls, mate," Mick said. "So, iss basically a caravan. You've gorra bed an' a little camp stove."

I stayed in there for six weeks, to be honest. It turned out alright for pullin', like. Honestly, the Lye is full of three things, Pakis, bikers an' slags.

Michelle

For someone as odd as Tim, an' for someone who'd bin through the wringer like 'im, 'e day 'alf 'av some attitude to people who was different. The old'uns were like it, but you could get that, they day know 'ow to be different, an' they day know 'ow to deal wi' change. An' they were freaks. Not freaks like Tim an' that – freaks who day know they was. So when the factories got closed, an' they day 'av nothin', an' no one seemed to wanna 'elp, an' the social club got boarded up 'cause no one was suppin', an loads 'a people on the 'ousin' list got screwed cause the council 'ouses got sold – but Sid was drivin' a BMW – it was all the fault 'a the *pakis*, wor it? I always knew it wor that simple but the Enoch Powell sorts was gerrin' big numbers 'round 'ere again, an' I know they love you to buy a scapegoat. Anyroad, we was mates wi' Shahid, an' there was Faisal an' Dipak an' the 'alf-caste kid wi' the spaz legs. I doh say 'alf-caste an' spaz anymore, but it used to be a shop, The Spastics did.

We gorr'on wi' it mainly, we wor saints, an' they was different than us, but we gorr'on wi' it. Tim day 'av an

73

excuse for being that way.

There wor no real reason for 'im to not goo home, for 'im to sort 'a live out theya. I s'pose Carrick wouln't 'av liked it much. But 'e wor thick, 'e couln't 'ave not 'eard all the stories, so 'e must've ignored 'em, 'an you gorr'a ask why then, doh ya? I doh think anyone 'ad the guts to tell the full story to him. See Carrick could be a cunt. 'E was a drunk an' a fighter, an' 'e'd bin inside. But 'e was loyal an' family was everythin'. I bet our Grandad'd said summat to 'im. No one 'ad the full story, mind. 'E wouln't 'a bin 'appy about Tim an' the pornos an' the boys. Tim'd probably 'ave gorra lampin' for it. But nothin' more than that. Maybe Carrick just day wanna admit it an' if 'e day do nothin', nothin' was outta place.

After the kickin', thass when Carrick turned in on 'imself. 'E was 'ard, an' you 'ad to be a bit careful. But 'e was sound too.

"Always gets a pint in, 'e does," Granddad said. "An' I remember when 'e dug the allotments out for Bernard and Trev, 'e did – they 'ad to force 'im to 'ave that twenty quid an' 'e only went an' shared it out in Pardoe's anyroad, day 'e."

'E wor never talkative, like, but 'e day look miserable or nothin'. You'd 'ave to watch your step with 'im 'cause 'e'd tek offense an' that'd be it. 'E'd gerr'is round in an' there'd be some small talk, an' 'e was good to know 'cause 'e sid everyone 'e knew as a friend 'a the family, an' in some ways we all wanted to be introduced as friends 'a the Carmodys'. But 'e went in on 'isself when

Tim got lamped. 'E wor the sem.

"'E's took 'is eggs to a fine market, 'e 'as," Grandad said. "Young Carmody, lef' 'is old mon between a rock an' 'ard place, 'e 'as. 'Ows 'e s'posed to act?"

'E wor never talkative but even chitchat stopped.

"'E doh talk with yo' no more, 'e talks at yo'. Sorta lamps yo' with 'e's stories. 'E's all bark now, Carrick is."

'E blamed us all, includin' Tim. See, 'e day know the truth an' I think somewhere in 'is 'ead 'e wanted to clout the fuck out 'a the lads who'd took Tim down, but 'e couln't, 'cause Tim an't come 'ome, an' thass a coward's way for Carrick, an' it meant mebe there was a reason for 'im runnin' off. So, Carrick wanted to knock the sin out 'a 'is son too. But 'e wanted 'im back too. An' 'e wanted revenge but 'e day know who to gi' it to. When 'e 'ad too much to drink 'e'd tell tall tales 'a wenchin', fightin', money. We'd all 'eard 'em, an' 'e was too drunk to end any story so 'e'd just keep sayin' the sem thing over an' over as if repeatin' would 'elp you realise 'is point.

"I gid 'im a fuckin' fish 'ook, I did, ar, gid 'im a fuckin' fish 'ook, ripped 'is cheek up to 'is lug 'ole, I gid 'im a fuckin' fish 'ook."

Gem called 'em Lager stories – the more Lager, the larger the story. S'pose 'e wanted to save face, but 'e day know fully what 'e was savin' it from. 'E was lost – that ay as simple as it sounds, 'cause you lose summat an' iss sort 'a in your control an' out of it too. If you lose yourself or get yourself lost, well, 'ow'd you get unlost, ow'd you re-find? Carrick'd become a drag thug. Mebe weem all drag versions of ourselves. Mebe weem all lost.

Tim

Honestly, I had all sorts back at the truck stop, that's
what I called it. Big men, old men, all sorts, like, an'
sometimes more than one, an' sometimes it'd be like a
little show, with them all around watchin, like.

It was just off the main road, so the traffic would be
gettin' on with its usual business, an' McDonalds an'
the BP Garage carried on the day to day. Just off the
main road, like, was a track – lightless, cut off with a
thick, rusty chain an' padlock. About a hundred metres
down was the yard, a tippin' ground for unwanted tat.
Piles of brittle exhaust pipes sat next to moss covered
fridges, next to mounds of black, torn tyres and towers
of moulding pallets. All this tat, neatly arranged, like.
Then the truck cab. My truck stop.

There was a pub up the road from the truck stop
where the bikers hung out. Mick 'ad introduced me,
like, when they came home from holiday. That's how
they knew what I was like. 'Cause Mick was, too. Most
of the bikers were just bikers, like, a solid group that'd
nod hello an' how do, pay their round at the bar, an'
watch your back as good as me dad would. But some
of the bikers were only dressed like bikers, you could
tell which 'cause they didn't have wear an' tear on their
boots an' jackets, like. That's when I learned about The
Leathers. Honestly, they taught me things.

Like, The Leathers had gestures an' symbols, an'

you had to learn 'em. Me an' Dave had picked some of 'em up from the toilet traders. The same rules applied with this lot. You day just come out an' say it, like. A carefully placed handkerchief, a particular colour, pokin' out of a specific pocket, that'd tell you all you needed to know. You needed a decent memory, like, the whole hanky code was complicated, I mean the gays ay just gonna have one shade of blue an' one shade of green, am they? Honestly, if you wor careful you'd be in for a proper surprise too – confuse lavender with magenta and you'd confuse drag with armpit fetish – not an easy ask in the corner of a dark pub, like. I was still a tourist then, most of 'em got that, most of 'em enjoyed it. I guess I still am, really like.

Honestly, it's more about a particular mood, a particular and peculiar sense. I don't want to end up in clubs like The Nightingale or Gorgeous, gettin' off with a twink while his girls from the salon giggle, *'cause iss nice to be out wi' the gays ay it, Trace, safe ay it. Eh, watch that dike, Trace, 'ers gorran' eye on ya.*

I don't want that, like. Don't want Disney Gay. Safe for the families, like. I want the accidental catchin' of a bloke tekkin' the shortcut past the bins, the lad who's parked up on the brown land where the chimneys used to pump four moons into the air. To be honest, iss more than just being gay, iss a gay that could only come from where we do.

Maybe it's self mythologisin', but what I'm gerrin' at 'as a point. It's easier to be gay now, they can 'av weddins' an' adopt kids an' everythin'. But with me, an' probably a lot of the others too, like, we day want that. There's a joy in the hidden, a love of bein' off-kilter, it wor necessarily swingin' an' not settlin' down but it wor based around suburbs an' all that. It doh 'av any pink pounds in it, an' in a big way, that meks all the difference.

Like, the Leathers had wives. They had kids an' cars an' jobs, some of them. To be honest, it was different down in the Lye. We'd get chattin' an' we'd have a few drinks, sometimes just two of us, sometimes a whole lot of us. We'd head back to the truckstop or we'd head over to the viaduct, like. Most people don't know but there's a cut off down Grayling Road that'll take you down an' past the Stour an' onto a bit of land, just behind the houses, where they'd be tuckin' their kids into bed. We'd find ourselves through a thicket of hawthorn, down a steep bank an' into a little openin'. Kids had made tree houses in the day. I sucked the fat cock of a fat Triumph rider by night.

Michelle

The bikers down Lye an' Quarry Bank were a big deal, they was great to get pissed with an' you'd 'av great fun wi' their heavy metal nights at The Lamp. Every now an' then you'd see a biker's funeral. You'd 'ear it fust – the low roar 'a slow movin' Triumphs. There was never any less than ten bikes in the procession, but mostly up in the twenties. It was a sight you day forget, an' it day get less impressive each time it 'appened.

"They stick together them lot, meks ya wanna weep," Nan'd say. "Yower dad was a biker, Gem. 'E'd goo from Wolverhampton to Bridgnorth on one 'ar'em low rider ones. Think they did it in fifteen minutes once too, bloody nutters."

There were certain rituals bikers did, they day spake much, well, they day say 'ow they felt, but a big bike parade to send someone off and a row 'a bandana crested 'eads bowed at church, that said more 'bout 'ow they felt.

The Wench behind the bar 'a Turner's was a biker, she used to be a whore. 'Er day talk about it. Why would you? But some 'a the old timers in Turner's u'd tell ya when they got drunk 'ow 'er used to turn tricks on the Hagley Road. Couple a bob a goo. Now, some 'a the old timers'd also tell you 'ow another wench on the game was Bella. 'Er was a favourite 'a some of 'em an' they noticed when 'er went missin'. I asked the landlady once when I got drunk enough to think it was alright.

"Doh believe all you 'ear, them lot ay got anythin' better to think on. Mind you, I wouln't get werritin' about Bella an' them woods, summats stuck in theya."

I day 'av no truck wi' that story really though. I mean, if you'd killed a prossie down on the Hagley road, you ay gonna carry 'er back to Netherton, am ya? You'd stick 'er in the Clent 'ills, wouln't ya? I needed to know an' I collected these stories.

Dave

The crank's useful at fust, but yo' soon find yo'self awake for too long. I doh think I can mek it out to the drop-in centre. I'm just too cold. My limbs. Every joint. I fuckin' creak, just sittin' still.

Just off the main road was a sort 'a driveway, cut off by a rusty chain. There was loads 'a tat. Machine parts an' old pipes an' rotten plasterboards. I went down an' hid in the corner. I was gonna get the fucker. That blister on me back's gonna pop, iss pussin'. *'E'd left. I day know 'e wor dead. At the one end was a lorry cabin. Thass where 'e was. 'E was theya with some little twink – messin' with each other.*

I ay bin to the bathhouse for a wik or two. I'm outta money. My feet wo' tek me theya – these jitters an' feelin' hot an' cold an' I doh know if I'm awake sometimes. Just at the back 'a the shop in Heathtown – I pay for the cubicle, the punters pay for me. Iss mucky but ... *I'd tell 'im. I was sat on a pile 'a corrugated tiles, damp an' covered in moss. I'd tell 'im. Doh yo' remember back at school, it was only ever us. Day yo' ever think. Tim, we 'ad summat? The real thing. We could 'ave gone away together. I thought it meant summat. I was just a prop up to ya, wor I? Now you've plopped me down. Yo' should see 'ow they look at me. I cor goo down Turner's or the 'ope. I'm locked out. Yo' did this. We 'ad summat. It wor just that once. Doh yo' remember? 'Oldin' 'onds through the woods? Huggin'? Bein' together. Proper together.* I'd sin gays on

80

the miner's march. It's turnin' around. *Jesus, Tim. I love yo'. What are yo' runnin' from?* From the outside the bathhouse was just a paki shop but when yo'm in the know yo' goo through the curtains at the back, an' yo'm in a space wi' a few little rooms, med up of MDF, there's a lightbulb, tarpaulin an' a sink. These fuckin' shivers – Tomo owes me – 'e pissed all over my blanket. *Tim finished that guy off an' I went over.*

"I'm spent kid, iss no good waitin'." 'E said. *But then he sid me. "Wass'up, Dave, iss bin ages."*

"No one knew where yow'd bin, Tim," I said. *I screamed arr'im. "We day 'ave a clue," it didn't goo to plan.* The puss, iss like mustard, it stinks. My jaw. My teeth. I need to sleep. *I wanted to win 'im over. I went right up to 'is face an' raised my fist. "Yow doh know what you've done to me, Tim, you cunt!"*

Joyce

I needed things to be in their place. Tim needed something as punishment. But I had to keep myself out of it all, too. Simon taught Chemistry and he'd only finished Uni about three months before. He was a kid himself and like a kid he loved to gossip. I'd heard him with the PE teachers at the Christmas meal. I'd seen him with Miss Simmonds on their cigarette break. Rumours would spread. All I had to do was accidently leave my logbook out on the desk, open at that day's page. He'd come and get registers for year nine and I'd turn my back on him for a minute too long. Simon saw

81

the entry – the stuff about Tim and the magazine and the toilets. I'd set it out perfectly – just enough detail to taint the boy, enough to make a mark and enough gaps to let the hearsay spread. It was safer dealing with it this way. I didn't want Carrick Carmody up here. I didn't want anything touching me. Nothing that close. Nothing that might second-guess, raise an eyebrow. I'm sorry. I still get it now. Closing up like I have is addictive.

Me and Yvonne were the queens of the gang and no one else bothered to challenge it. Most nights were the same really. We met up on Cinder Bank, hung about at St Andrew's cemetery for a bit, then walked down Lodge Hill Farm and into Saltwells. We got into a habit of walking around, smoking, sometimes drinking. The others would run off ahead, mucking around while me and Yvonne strutted along.

"We'll get a little place together," I said. "When we finish school."

"In America, Joyce. Get outta this dump an' get to where iss 'appenin'."

"And you can marry Johnny Cash."

"Ar. Thass it. An' I'll 'ave 'is babbies an' we'll drink milkshakes an' there wo' be any piece work for us."

"Too right, Yvonne."

We started spending more and more time away from Ernie and the others. We'd hold back and let them play about. That's when we became more. We were only about fourteen but we spent so much time planning, and seriously planning, too.

"We'll breeze the exams," I told her. "I can help you with the science ones. Mom and Dad'll help with the sewing and stuff. Then we can get teaching jobs in Chicago, New York, Boston, Washington. And we can move around every few years."

"An' we'll stick together, wo' we, Joyce? An' we'll be the fust ones to 'ear the new music an' goo to the roundhouse."

"And marry a couple of writers or journalists or filmmakers."

"Ar, an' live next door an' on Satdees we'll tek the babbies to Coney Island."

It all sounds like childish girl talk but we were serious at the time. Looking back now, it wouldn't have been that difficult to do. It still isn't, I suppose.

"It'll be yo' and me, our Joyce. Out theya in New Orleans. Tharr'll gi' 'em a cog knowler to chew on. Wo' it? We'll gerr'a little apartment, Joyce, eh? Work in a high school. Eat Creole Stew. Ar, no more pieces 'a licka for tay. The American dream."

She'd started giving me a hug goodnight. She'd walk me back to the Dudley bus stop and wait with me. She'd fling her arms around my neck and squeeze.

"Tara'abit, bab."

Yvonne came over to mine a few times for tea. We never went to hers.

"Dad works shifts and we cor wake 'im and them bastards anyway," she always said.

My mom and dad let her stay the night a few times. They loved her. You wouldn't have thought it really, being the coolest and most rock and roll of all of us, but she knew how to turn it on and off. She knew how to be the best girl in front of parents.

"Thank you, Mrs Wyatt. That's a lovely necklace, Mrs Wyatt."

She was smart, too, which helped. My parents knew Cinder Bank, and there were loads of people who knew us so they felt safe with that. Yvonne knew how to be polite and could talk about school and stuff. She had plans, like me, my parents liked that.

Mom worked nights so only really saw Yvonne on a Sunday, after she'd stopped the night. We had breakfast and then we dropped her back before church. The rest of the time it was us and Dad.

"It's good to see you again, Yvonne," Dad said. "I'm heading out to get some wild garlic down on the common." He gave me a wink. "There's a trout in the larder – I caught yesterday down Green Pool. Help yourself."

"Thanks Mr Wyatt," Yvonne said. We both gave him a little smirk. He smiled back.

"Maybe the three of us can go out sometime, eh? We'll show you what we can do, Yvonne?"

Dad was lovely. He knew I still wanted to collect berries and duck eggs with him, but he knew I was a different sort of Joyce when Yvonne was around. He was great. He got it. He'd make us tea and stuff but that was that.

We spent less and less time with the gang. We used to spend a few nights down in Netherton and then a few at mine in Penn. I think she liked it at ours. Mom would always do sausage and mash or cottage pie. She loved being the host. Dad liked to see me with a friend. She'd stop over on a Friday night and stay to watch Big Daddy and Giant Haystacks on the TV on Saturday. Like I said, we spent a lot of time planning. We had a massive scrapbook of our plans. Cut outs from magazines and catalogues and all our scribbles about what we were going to do. Mom and Dad just laughed but we were deadly serious. It didn't last that long, and it never worked out.

Dad used to take me to Bilston Market. I loved it there. It was always full of people rushing about and hollering to each other. It looked crazy. People looked crazed. But if you knew it, you knew. Between the charge and scrum of shoppers you'd see the quick pat on the back, rub on the arm, handshake. If you cut through the sounds you could break up the shouts between Tuppence for ya opples, tuppence fer ya pears, and, 'Ow do Frank, your Rose back on 'er feet? I got a Johnny Cash LP for Yvonne.

"Joyce! Bloody 'ell Bab! I love it, iss great, that."

That's the first time she kissed me. A hug and a quick peck on the cheek. That little giggle.

"Happy Birthday, Yvonne." I said.

"Cheers Bab. Weem really gonna do this, ay we? We ay like the rest on 'em, am we? Yo'm great."

I knew what she meant. The rest were mates – muckers. We were different. She'd only ever hugged me before.

I sort of grew out of the foraging stuff with dad.

Yvonne

I day 'alf love that Johnny Cash LP. I felt a little stomach turn on that. I did hug 'er proper that day. I was med up. Thing is, 'er wor on the level. I'd sin Mom an' Nan an' me sister just doin' the sem old shit over an' over. Like if yo'm born on Cinder Bank yo' ay got no choice. I s'pose this was trainin, in a way. An' I s'pose if 'er could gerr'us to America I'd lerr'er. I was gerr'in out. Joyce'd teach us 'ow to hold my knife an' fork an' tell us about the stuff at the wenches school then I'd gerr'out.

I day feel good all the time. Iss a strange feelin'. Yo' sorta feel a tickle from it an' yo' cor separate the thrill from the guilt. Mr an' Mrs Wyatt was dead nice. Generous.

It was a beautiful day when we went to the Stourton Lido. I'd bin out in the yard a few days before an' I was lookin' good. Sunkissed. There was only me in a bikini an' I sid the dads all lookin', an' I sid Joyce see the dads, too. People care when yo' doh care. It was fun. Doh get me wrong, 'er was a nice wench an' they was a nice family. Nice ay gettin' the babby a new bonnet. Yo've gotta kip an eye on the aim. Be like Margot Shelby in Decoy. I'd sid 'ow 'er looked up at me.

Eric was talkin' to me once.

"I thought maybe me an' yo' could, yo' know, if yo' want," 'e said. I just looked arr'im. Raised my eyebrow. I giggled a little but I was 'opin' tharr'd purr'im off.

"She doesn't want to," Joyce told 'im. 'Er just stepped in. It gets to yo' that does. Feels good. Yo' wanna see 'ow much yo' can bend it.

Tim

Dave'd come an' found me one night, down the truck stop, like. Said he'd bumped into Nicki and Mick. I was busy, you know. I think there was me an' another fella who wanted me to fuck him, kept sayin' he wasn't gay, an' was married, an' just did it sometimes. Honestly, I wasn't bothered, he looked like Mickey Rourke. I saw this guy watchin' us, like, from out near the big pile of railway sleepers. That wasn't that odd, people did that sometimes. But this guy stuck around after Mickey Rourke had gone. He just sat there, like.

"I'm spent kid, iss no good waitin'," I shouted. Then he came up to the cab, like. It was Dave. 'E was shiverin', snivelin'. I called out to him.

"Wass'up, Dave, iss bin ages."

"No one knew where yow'd bin, Tim," He screamed. "We day 'ave a clue."

Honestly, he came right up to my face and raised his fist. He was in bits.

"Yow doh know what you've done to me, Tim, you cunt!"

Then he legged it, like. That's the last time I saw him, to be honest. I didn't give him much thought around that time an' I wasn't too bothered. All that was in the past, like, an' I'd moved on. I could do with another chance at it, really.

I'd been stayin' at the truck stop for about five weeks, an' I'd settled in to this little life. These people loved a good fuck, like, but they were tender, decent people too. They'd say 'ow am ya bab? You eatin' alright? Our Sylv's gorr 'er stew extra for ya, our kid, an' 'ers fixed ya jumper up, an all. Honestly, they were a tight bunch, an' they'd introduce you to all sorts, other Bikers in Wolves or Telford. So you'd always be chattin' with the cousin of a mate or someone who knew Mick when they went 'round Scotland in the sixties.

One night a chap we called Welsh John led me through to the back room of the pub an' there she was. She didn't see me straight off, like, she was chattin' with a couple of others. Then she did that thing people do, like – she looked down at her glass an' moved her hair to one side, an' as she did her eyes caught mine for a second, she looked away then looked back, then pretended she hadn't seen me, like. But I kept lookin' an' about five seconds after, she looked again.

Honestly, I wanted to pull 'er apart, but I day. Part of me was froze. Part of me knew that if Miss Wyatt 'ad med it to this pub in Lye, and med it in biker gear, then 'er knew some people who wouldn't want me smashin' 'er in the face, like. An' 'er would've known the sem too.

Now that she'd seen me an' she knew that I knew we'd both seen each other, there was no ignorin' it. She finished up her chattin' with the others then came over.

"I hadn't expected to see anyone from school in this

place," she said.

"You've got a nerve comin' to this pub," I told 'er. "An' another nerve to talk with me."

Her left hand, just on the knuckle, 'ad the stretched, pale plastic look of scar tissue.

"Cigarette? Pint?"

"That's the least you can do."

To be honest, it wor a beer garden, it was a six by six patch of land with a buncha broken pavin' stones as a patio an' a wooden bench that'd creak under anyone's weight. A rusted caravan an' a wet mattress dumped in the corner. Like the garden at Turners, but at least the wench behind the bar 'ad built a sorta bus shelter. No one needed a beer garden then though, the cunts 'adn't stopped us smokin' everywhere back then, like.

The biker's pub was built for us really. I liked those old man's pubs too though, especially on an afternoon. Loadsa people find 'em depressin' but I doh. Them old men 'ave summat blue about 'em, like, but they've made the pub lounge a sorta sanctuary. Doh forget, they're freaks, a bit like me I s'pose. But they're proper freaks, no pretendin', they doh even know 'ow strange they are. They'd get upset out of nothin'. Spend ages talkin' about their teas. Their laughter sounds like a train breakin'.

I remember one old timer in Turner's once, 'e'd 'ad a fall an' 'is face was all cut up, an' 'e was cryin', like.

"Ah use to be one of the 'ardest men in Dudley." That's all 'e said. That's all 'e 'ad, like. 'E was in bits about it. "Ah use to be one of the 'ardest men in

Dudley," 'e just kept sayin' it. 'E's creased face an' bloodshot eyes, 'e's twitchin' lip, 'e's furrowed brow – looked like 'e'd lost everythin', like. There's a lot of it 'round 'ere, to be honest. Men who day figure out what to be next when the windows started gerrin boarded up an' the rules changed.

You'd hear 'em say faggot or nigger or chinky, but they never bothered no one about it as long as you day bother them with it, like. It ay perfect but . . .

They're nothing like me, but it's easy here. I nod an' say hello. They nod back. We're not the same people, like, but it's manners before morals.

The biker's pub was best, like. We were completely safe there.

"I think I owe you an apology," Wyatt said.

"An' then some."

"There's some stuff I need to explain."

Bella

I can't piece it together. Can't fully make a picture from these senses. I said it was like a smell. Like the smell that electrifies through the body. The incense at St Andrew's on a Sunday. Dad's beer breath. Mom's carbolic soap. I taste it and I don't know if I should relish in it. It sits just out of view – a blurred spot in the corner of your eye – and every time you turn to see it, it's gone. You don't know if it's a devil or a guardian. That's how it is.

90

You step into the woods and you step away from the path. That's when you start to notice. Away from the normal routes the things you hear become more, and it becomes more for you that you can't see what makes it. The fidget of animals. The insect buzz. On the path you'd shake it off, but here, with me, you can't be sure. It's a throb. The throb grows with each step closer to the Wych-Elm. Most of you turn back early. Some of you make it to the tree. Some of you see me. You call me Bella and you know I see you.

There are two boys who come to me. They come unafraid. Not totally unafraid – less so. I see them grab at each other and kiss. They rub hungry hands over each other. They bite lips and scratch at backs. I see one take a cock in his mouth and spend delicate moments sucking, licking thrusting pelvis into face. They look at each other and small smiles curl in the corner of their mouths. They stroke each other's cheek. They kiss. They kiss over and over. They are starved and each is a feast for the other.

The first time I saw them they were dancing. They'd been drinking. They took it in turns. They lay on the damp earth and cuddled. With heavy breath, sweat dripping, curled up in each other's limbs. I saw it all. At one moment they must have seen too. They must have half seen or sensed me seeing. Something startled them. They dressed and rushed off.

I like to see them. They got used to the woods. I think they got used to my stare. They come back often to love each other.

91

6

Michelle

I'd read reports about Bella. Old newspapers and police statements. Iss always vague, just details. Some weird ones though. I 'ad to know. I collected 'em. When them scouts found 'er, 'er 'ad a wad 'a taffeta stuck in 'er mouth. In the mouth 'a the skull. They found one shoe an' bits 'a 'er clothes. They say 'er 'ad distinctive teeth, warr'ever that means. There was one 'and they never found. Still stuck theya 'idden in the Saltwells woods more than likely. One 'and.

"The hond of glory," Nan'd say. "The Black Sabbath priests'd cut theya hond off an' then they could summon the power of the dead. They'd stick the body in the Wych-Elm to keep the spirit locked up."

Miss Wyatt caught me runnin' to English once.

"Plenty of energy you have there, perhaps we need to transfer it to a more suitable place though, hmm?" 'Er said.

'Er 'ad me meet 'er at the sports 'all, 'ad to get changed into kit from lost property – 'er stood theya watchin' me struggle into shorts too small and a stinkin' rugby top, 'er watched with 'er stern look on 'er face, tappin' 'er index finger to 'er dimpled chin like 'er was twitchin' an' impatient. 'Er day tek 'er eyes off me 'til I'd wrestled into the kit.

Then 'er med me do two laps 'a the sports field. The wust was, it was lunch time so everyone sid me an' every one 'ad a proper loff an' really took the piss. Even Shahid took the piss, an' that was before 'e med the gang. It was wuss than that too, though. It was lunch, and the sports field went past the Staff Room, an' Mr Bragg 'ad sin me an' 'e come out to see if I wanted to be in the cross country team, an' Miss Wyatt said that'd be a great idea, an' 'er gid me a look like – Doh you dare get cute wi' me! – so I 'ad to join the fuckin' cross country team, an' all I wanted to do was hang about the cut, get the older lads to gerr'a bottle 'a twenty-twenty, smoke some 'a the SuperKings Shahid nicked from Sheena's, an' get off wi' James Hadley. An' maybe let 'im slip a cheeky finger. I think 'e liked Gem though, but 'er day care about boys, never did.

Nan'd said 'er was a queer one too, Wyatt was. 'Er day mean it like we mean it now. Nan wor into rock an' roll and all that leather shit. Nan day 'av time. She was either 'elpin' down the allotments, doin' the washin', or at the pictures. Pictures were Nan's thing.

"Satdee afternoon me an' our Sue'd goo down the Plaza, we would, ar. You'd watch cartoons, the news an' a film back then, bag 'a chips on the way 'ome, an' wid look over our shoulders an' quick step past all the gullies all the way 'ome if we'd sin a Lon Cheyney picture, we would ar."

Nan'd say 'ow Wyatt was at school too. "'er was a bully, 'er 'ad ways of meking you miserable that no one else knew about, 'er did, ar."

'Er was a fucker at our school too, but it was different, most teachers were fuckers an' ya cor tell properly when y'am a kid an' them old.

Nan day 'ave rose tinted specs, she saw it 'ow it was. 'Er told us about it comin' back from Merry Hill one weekend.

"Back at school, er wor 'alf a cow, 'er was, ar," Nan said. "'Er day start out like it, it was the last few years really. I was one of three girls from our area to get picked, the other two wor from our estate so I day know 'em anyroad, I day. There were wenches from Wolves, Kingswinford, Wombourne – all over the Wrekin' – some of 'em was like us, 'ard workin' an' smart but our dads did shifts at Roundoak or Goodyears. Most of 'em, mind, were nasty little bitches, they was, ar. Wyatt was like that."

"What did she do?" I asked.

"Just med us stand out, bab. Stand out both ends. Mom knew 'ow to grow an' pick spuds, 'er knew 'ow to mek Dad's wage last us, 'er knew 'ow to clean the

95

bar at The Bull, 'er knew 'ow to play the church organ, or anythin' with keys, 'er did, ar. 'Er knew wharr'er needed to, an' wharr'er needed to know about, 'er knew inside out, 'er did, ar. My old mon was the sem, 'e was supervisor at Roundoak, 'ad a shift of twenty blokes under 'im, 'e knew 'is trade inside out, 'e did, ar. I day. I day know a thing. I day 'av to know. An' the more time I 'ad doin' Latin an' Pythagoras instead of 'elpin' on the allotment, the more I was cut away from 'em."

"So they thought yo' was posh, Nan?"

"It wor no different the other way neither, it wor. They 'ad me doin' me sums, lookin' at Shakespeare an' photosynthesis – an' I was good arr'it, I was, ar. I wor no dummy. But I day get anywhere near the top. See, to them, I was the lucky poor girl who'd 'ope to be a typist if I ever managed to gerr'a new dress. I was gonna be a spy, I was, ar. Undercover cold war code breaking – thass wharr'I'd do, I would, ar. To them, no matter 'ow well I knew me conjugations, I was still a wench who cor spayke proper. I was just a little too smart for me mates from Derby End, a little too mucky for the grammar girls."

Our Gem said similar stuff to Nan:

"Weem judged on 'ow we spake an' where weem from," 'er said. "I cor 'elp geography an' I ay gonna fuckin' start spakin' different."

"Doh get me wrong," Nan said. "It wor like I was on me own an' no one understood me or nothin'. We was marked out a bit, thass all an' even if thass a small crack, it ay one that you can weld shut, it ay."

I remember our Gem sayin' summat similar, about only feelin' fully okay with 'erself when 'er was on the Delph with 'er girls. Gem knew pretty early in 'er life tharr'er liked girls, 'er told me fust 'cause we day 'av secrets. Weem twins, ay we, Gem? 'Er loved me and 'er loved me nan and granddad, 'it wor that 'er wor 'erself with us. But iss like Nan says, if there's a crack, it ay gerrin' fixed, it doh have to ruin everythin', it just is. Gem felt the cracks less when 'er was with 'er girls on the Delph. When 'er was fifteen, sixteen, 'er day know where to goo, there wor anywhere 'round 'ere 'er could try out bein' a lezza. 'Er went to Brum a couple 'a times, to the big clubs on Thursdays, but it day work. I like girls, but I ay a dike like them lot, I doh know the rules. Gem needed a bunch 'a lesbians, a sisterhood 'er called it, but 'er needed a bunch who 'ad the same sense 'a division that 'er'd spotted. 'Er ended up gerr'in a job at the Tenth Lock, through a friend of a friend, Gem said they sort 'a knew each other back at school, sort 'a knew to look out for each other. After that you couln't gerr'er away. There was a gang of about eight lesbians, who in their own way, ruled the Delph run. It wor easy. It wor completely safe. But they all 'ad that edge to 'em. Skirts from the outskirts, Tim called 'em.

There was a wench called Jess on the Delph. 'Er granddad was in the war too, 'e did four years on the front in France an' then worked in some secret division in Brum.

"So, 'e knew a Dutch spy who 'ad a wife called Arabella or summat," Jess said. "So, 'er 'ad bad teeth

97

an' a funny way about 'er. Me grandad said 'e met 'er once but soon after that the Dutch stopped talkin' about 'er. Me grandad always knew that bloke 'ad got rid of 'er, 'e'd stuffed 'er in the trunk of a tree in Saltwells. So, 'e never proved it. An' yo' know. We doh goo in theya."

Nan'd say Wyatt wor too bad in the fust few years. They wor friends but they wor enemies neither.

"We knew each other well enough, we did, ar," Nan said. "To nod 'ello to, but that was it really. I remember you'd see 'er down the Bilston Market, always with 'er old mon, 'oldin' 'onds, 'er was. 'Er looked dead 'appy, 'er did, ar. It wor until we was in the last few years tharr'er changed."

"That 'appens all the time at our school, Nan," I said. "It ay nothin' major, just summat over the six wiks 'olidees an' someone's different."

"Joyce Wyatt was top class, top of every class; sport, singin', maths, science, the lot. 'Er was teachers' favourite, 'er was, ar. 'Er was prefect. 'Er was clever an' all that but 'er wor a swat, people liked 'er in them fust few years, people wanted to be liked by 'er. Then, in the September of our third year theya 'er changed, 'er did, ar. 'Er was still top of class, still 'ead of the choir and captain in hockey, but 'er day nod 'ello to us anymore, 'er looked down on us, 'er did, ar. 'Er'd changed, 'er did. 'Er was cold an' we all 'ad to earn 'er mercy. I day know warr'appened, no one did. Just at the beginning of that year Joyce 'ad changed an' we all knew straight away."

"I know what yo'm sayin', Nan. We all changed so much durin' school an' the six wik 'olidays were a lifetime back then so sometimes we'd come back to school as different people. You day 'ave to 'ave any story, any big event that med you, you just changed."

Shahid never said a word about what 'appened when 'e got lost in Saltwells. Obviously we all begged 'im an' begged 'im but 'e just kept sayin 'e day know.

"It doh matter 'ow often you aks me," 'E said. "Ah cor tell ya. It ay that ah woh say, ah cor say. Ah got through the thicket an' past the clay pits, Ah cut through into the openin' an' ah sid the Wych-Elm ... Then me dad and yower grandad was shekin' me an' pullin me out. Yower grandad aksed my dad not to look, 'e said you could feel it lookin' but ya never look back."

Grandad day tell us much, 'e just med us promise to never goo back in.

Nan'd say, "it doh matter 'ow many times yo' ask 'im, 'e ay never gonna tell us what was lookin' an' what yo' shouln't look back at, 'e woh. Now come an' 'av ya tay." An' 'er'd med me an' Gem's sausage, egg an' chips into a witch's face.

'Er loved it, Nan did. 'Er used to tek me an' Gem up to the pictures at Merry 'ill when we was old enough to get into fifteens an' eighteens.

"Iss stupid any road, these age things, it is, ar. I'm ya Nan an' I say iss alright to watch monsters an' ghosts even if yow am younguns."

An' 'er used to tell the lad at the counter if 'e asked us for ID too, only 'er'd say 'er knew 'is nan, an' 'er wouln't be too 'appy if 'er knew 'ow 'e'd spoke to 'er. An' 'er used to goo to the video shop too an' get classics out, 'er loved Vincent Price so we'd watch *The Fly, The Bat, The 'Ouse of Usher* every six wiks. An' when Michael Jackson's *Thriller* come out, bloody 'ell.

"Stan, Stan, 'av yow 'eard this, Stan. Iss our Gem's new tape, iss got Vincent Price on it, ay it! Remember Stan, when we met at the Grand, we did, ar, an' yow took me to the pictures, yo' did, ar, an' we watched Karloff, Chaney and then Price?"

Grandad med a noise an' smiled.

"An' 'e was from Dudley, 'e was ar," Nan'd tell us. "That bloke who med Frankenstein, wor 'e? That James Whale, 'e was a Queer, 'e was, ar."

'Er loved James Whale though, really. Nan'd say, "he's a queer but e's alright." 'Er'd tek us up to where 'e lived as a kid, 'is old schools in Kate's 'ill an' Dixon's Green.

"'E med summat of 'imself, 'e did, ar, like Duncan Edwards but better, 'e med the most important horror film ever, 'e did, ar an' look at the state of it round 'ear, it was wuss when Whale was a lad too, it was, ar."

Nan'd say, "play that tape again, our Gem," an' 'er'd try an' do the moves wi' us, an' when Vincent Price came on 'er'd do 'er best impression, 'er loved it so much 'er'd learnt all the words, an' wid roll around loffin'.

"'E was a beautiful lad when 'e was a kid, 'e was, ar, dead handsome for a darky, even on that last one with blame it on the moonlight, 'e was good lookin'. Yow cor tell if 'e ay a wench these days, yo' cor."

Nan was mint, 'er still is. There's a new place in Stourbridge now what puts movies on. Creepy Sparrow they call it, iss lovely, different from Turner's an' the 'ope. It 'as bands on an' local artists put theya paintins up, an' all the boys 'av got beards an' tattoos, an' they love wax jackets an' old jumpers, an' if yow'd sin a film the'd sin it before it 'ad come on the TV. The wenches were sound though, they just liked it that everyone liked stuff. It ay always horror they put on, but whenever it is, me and Gem'll tek Nan up. An' the wench behind the bar'd save Nan the big leather sofa. Gem copped off wi' 'er once, said 'er was a kinky bugger, used to 'av our Gem dress up in lace an' stockins an' just rub 'em. 'Er was from Cradley so 'er 'ad the sem landscape as us, old dormant factories an' empty social clubs. So it was probably the sem reason Tim was like 'e was too, nowhere else to goo that was safe to find your place in stuff. Tim liked it theya, 'e liked the wench too – they got each other.

Tim

This was the nineties, like, now we'd grown up a bit, an' lots had already been done but for quite a lot of people we were still weirdos – an' if you threw AIDS in the mix, honestly, we were fuckin' dangerous. AIDS was still lingerin' an' it did well into the nineties. An' *Queer as Folk* had bin on the TV, but that was Manchester, like, an' they had a Gay Village. It wor The Lye, it wor Quarry Bank. Honestly, we didn't have the same safe places an'

101

that's why we were a different sort to them.

Mick an' Nicky were bostin'. All the bikers were bostin'. With our lot, it was more about bein' off kilter, like. Some of them wor nothin', to be honest. Just different. They were married folks – maybe they liked to share, maybe they liked to watch, maybe they liked to be mothered or smothered or whatever. It didn't matter. The bikers didn't let anyone get between you, an' they didn't judge.

If I'd told anyone, Wyatt'd have been ruined. She'd already retired but it would still have made her life awkward, like. She'd made my life awkward so I owed her one really, an' I was fuckin' angry but I couldn't get Mick's voice out my head. *We've gorr'a look out for each other, ay we? There ay many on us about.*

I decided I'd keep my mouth shut.

"I still have nightmares. Most nights that Wych-Elm appears in my dreams," she said.

Honestly, Saltwells wor frightenin' to me. We'd play war in the woods when we were little, play cowboys an' Indians, like. Dad'd always have me back before dark anyway, an' I wor gonna get a hidin' for bad time keepin'. More than this like. Saltwells was where me and Dave 'ad sex, not just the first time but times after, too. Other than the odd dog walker, no one'd go in the spaces we went to, especially after Shahid like, so we had full rein of the place. Honestly, we'd goo a couple of times a week. We longed for it. We'd spend hours kissin' an' touchin' each other, he used to touch my neck an' chest, he was soft like, gentle. Then we'd fuck

102

or have a quick tug off an' head home. We'd go back to Saltwells all the time but sometimes it wasn't like that. Doh get me wrong, when we were fifteen – sixteen, like, a couple of times a week, at least, we'd get our ends away with each other. We were teenagers and it was always 'iverin' over us. Sometimes though, especially when it got dark like, an' it was cold, we'd just have a stroll. We'd walk around just holdin' hands. Nothin' more. Sometimes we didn't even speak, to be honest. Just walked about holdin' hands. It was just us an' the woods and the night time.

"Yo' two'll get square fuckin' eyes," Dad'd say. 'Cause we kept gooin' to the cinema, 'cause it was dark. It was too public an' too normal there, but we'd hold hands through the film, like, and I'd see him look over at me an' grin sometimes too, an' we'd both get hard-ons an' have to walk back through Saltwells. So, Saltwells for me was lovely. Honestly, it was filthy, but it was lovely. I hope it was the same for Dave. I wish I'd told him. We really had our moments there.

It was filthy for Wyatt too, she hadn't been in for donkey's years, it was a constant threat to her, an' she couldn't stop dreamin' it.

Joyce

Simon let it spill to the rest of the science teachers. There was nothing too much to tell. Just enough to have him treated differently. Enough for all of them to notice.

I left some advice for the prefects, too.

"Watch that Carmody lad at break time," I told them. "Keep an eye on him, especially if he drifts off out of sight."

"'Ow come, Miss?"

"We need to make sure he's not up to anything . . . anything improper."

That kind of thing lingers. Lingering – like a migraine you can't place the root of. I knew what I was by then. I knew it by the time the Sixties had come and gone. But it still needed keeping in check. I suppose I overreacted. But if that sex stuff, that organ quiver feeling, that empty stomach feeling came over me, I just locked it out and locked myself away from it. I could have done things by the book and had his parents up. I could have just left it. I suppose I learnt some of it from Yvonne. But I was torn. There was duty and there were secrets to keep.

I never felt the urge to kiss a girl. Never felt it before Yvonne, anyway. I don't even think it was a sexual thing really. I just thought she was beautiful. She was utterly beautiful. And bit by bit she became mine. She hugged me. Then there was the kiss. She had a way of looking at me, made me feel strange. *Good* strange. We got closer and closer. You had to come through me to get to her, even if it was simply asking her for a cigarette, I was the gatekeeper. The closer we got the more mine she became, the more mine she became the more I wanted to kiss her. I wanted to possess, I suppose. I wanted to consume. I wanted her to myself, wanted us to merge,

that's the only way you keep something to yourself –
you make it part of you.

We'd known each other for about a year and been
really close for about six months. We were best friends.
Sisters. We had plans to conquer America. Sometimes I
saw her looking at me for a moment longer than normal.
Taking me in. We finished each other's sentences.

We were as close as close could be. One night we
went to the Penn cinema. I remember it vividly. We
went to see *The Belles of St Trinian's*. Not exactly
Citizen Kane and not our usual, too cool for school
type thing but we liked it and we were together so it
was fine. One thing we both loved was Arabella, she
was the rebel. She'd been expelled from school and
was now back to try and rip off a rich Sultan. She had
a sort of tomboy swagger about her we both liked. We
had popcorn and coke. We held hands through the
whole thing. We held hands a lot. It wasn't like that.
Well ... I don't know. We held hands through the
whole film and we were really close. It felt good.
Special.

She was stopping at mine that night, Penn cinema
wasn't far from ours. Mom made us pikelets for tea and
we were allowed to eat in bed. We shared the bed. We
stopped up talking until midnight.

"The girls at school are different," I told her. "They're
all square. All of them. Not like us. They didn't get it
and they don't get us and they'll never do anything with
their lives."

"Thass right, Joyce," she said. "Weem on the level,

ay we?"

"I hate it. Can't wait 'til it's over. There's only the hockey for me these days. I'm the queen of the hockey pitch."

"I bet yo' am."

"The others are all terrified of me."

It mattered to me then. It makes me embarrassed a bit now. It's something I couldn't get rid of really – I needed that control. I still do, I suppose. I'm sorry. I've tried very hard but some things you just can't shake.

Sheena

We couldn't get used to it when we first moved from Lahore. Evil eye, we say *Buri Nazar*. Not just the cold. Not just the food. Alleys – gulleys they call them – cut-out routes through most places and most times you move from the off-white, pebbledash of the Priory estate, into the tall slate and ash of dormant factory works, and then into the slick clay, weeds, nettles and brittle trees of somewhere like Wren's Nest Nature Reserve. Nothing like the Punjab. These sites were all over. In-between sites where you can't be sure if nature is dying from all the old smog, or if it is slowly working its way back. We know there's no killing it, there's no stopping it. It's bad, haram, buri nazar, the evil eye. It's like the flu, you can go to Dr Patel's but he isn't going to stop snot coming out your nose, you can build new posh houses but the foxgloves won't quit churning up the bricks. It's a Kuti – a dog. It's bigger

106

than us, it's older than us and it'll be here long after us. *Buri Nazar.*

When we first moved in, and unpacked everything, every single clock in the house stopped working. We had about five clocks and they all stopped. Not at the same time but within a day of each other. They *all* stopped.

Then, after about a week there was a wet patch on the wall in the bedroom. Only a small one. Sid peeled back the wallpaper and damp had seeped through the plaster. Just that one spot though. We checked the room below and the one next to it and there was nothing – just this little patch of wet that came through the plaster. It didn't sink down or spread through or nothin'. We got the Imam in from Lye. He says, sometimes spaces tek a time to settle around changes. Sometimes they doh. Sometimes they never do.

Sid never spoke about Shahid and the woods. You'd overhear customers talking about Bella and people getting trapped in old pits. It took Sid a whole day to scrub the wall of the shop when someone had spray-canned *Who put Bella down the Wych-Elm.*

That's what it's like round here – *badsoorat*, ugly – they built this area over centuries worth 'a dead oceans, fossils, pit holes, forges – *Buri Nazar*. It still isn't used to the new wallpapers we stick up over the old ones.

Bella

She led me by the hand through this. Her arm outstretched and pulling me away from the pebbled path. Through nooks of bushes. Through gaps in trees. You wouldn't know they were there. All is shadow. Memory is difficult. Every stump, plant, ditch or rise, cloaked in the thin crepuscular lace. She led me by the hand through this. Her soft hand leading me. All is quiet – not silent. It is absent of normal sound. Only our footsteps. Only our breath. We are alone here. We are away from our homes. There is no clank and churn or purr of forges, furnaces and machines. There is no mumble of voices. All is quiet – not silent. Just the flutters, scurries, snaps and cracks of the woods and the shy creatures that stow away here.

I saw her look at me from across the bar. She sipped brandy and pep. She smiled. I didn't know what I was doing there. I don't know why I went back the next week. I saw her look again. She sipped brandy and pep. I saw her smile. I'd returned and we both knew that was currency.

Blonde hair, bobbed, cut around the frame of her face. Ashen skin. Red lips. Her nose had been broken once. Eyes – the colour of the cut – secrets. She wore a blue dress. It was a little tight on her. The same dress as last week. I'd returned and we both knew that was currency.

Memory is difficult. She asked me questions and giggled at me. Her giggle stood out too. I don't remember it all. We spoke of things and she giggled. She touched my hand for a second. We had another drink. I don't remember it all. She said she liked my shirt. I had it tied at the waist with a yellow ribbon. She asked about it and giggled. We had another drink. She touched my hand. She held it.

I'd done it before. I thought of Carol from the Ambulance Corps.

She led me by the hand through this. I don't remember it all. Memory is difficult. She led me by the hand to the Wych-Elm. She turned me around and pressed my back against it. She became ravenous. I was supple. Eyes closed, mouth wide. Soft, moist movements of tongue and lips slipped slowly over neck, shoulder. One hand pinned my arms above my head, held fast against the trunk of the tree. One hand unbuttoned my shirt. Soft, moist movements of tongue and lips slipped slowly down. Slowly became sucks, nibbles. One hand gripped my thigh. She eased my skirt up. She ripped at tights. Wrestled a hand into knickers. Touched cunt.

My arms broke free and reached for her – running fingers through hair, down neck and spine. We didn't notice how cold it was. She teased – delicate and firm. Teased me into becoming nothing but that moment. She made me pure – nothing existed outside the throb, the stroke, the tickle, the tease. I collapsed into it. She led me. I collapsed. Ravenous. Heaven.

7

Michelle

Dave joined the army. Well, 'e signed up. 'E day actually mek it. Day even mek it to trainin'. After Tim went off with Mick an' started livin' down on the industrial estate an' muckin' about wi' the bikers, Dave day know what to do. 'E wor as weird as Tim. 'E knew a bit more wharr'e wanted. 'E just day know 'ow to goo about gerrin' it wi' the sem verve as Tim. 'E started gerrin the 297 to Wolves on an evening. Started 'angin' out at the bars. Started doin' crystal meth and sellin' isself to gerr'it. Before the trainin'd start in the army 'e 'ad to do a physical. They tested 'is blood an' that was it. It wor the drugs that bothered 'em. Summat to do with dendritic cells.

We didn't go to the funeral. That idea from school, that silly idea that we'd get infected. Everyone just

111

forgot about him.

I read once, in A-Levels at Halesowen College, we did a bit on this tribe in Africa. When a girl became a woman, when 'er 'ad 'er blob, 'er was sent to a separate hut well away from the rest 'a the tribe. 'Er 'ad to stay theya until it was done. 'Every wench 'ad to goo, every time 'er was on. Our teacher said it was a mix 'a stuff. They was afraid 'a blood 'cause blood meant illness an' death. They was afraid 'a the blood 'cause blood was magic. But more than that, it was sex too. The women 'ad become sexed. The women 'ad blood coming from the bits where sex 'appened. So these wenches were both powerful, to the rest of 'em, an' also weak. They might get a spell cast on 'em, or they might get sick. It was summat they 'ad to get to a safe space. Iss like that with the others too. We send 'em off to a safe space, either ignore 'em or cast 'em out. We think it stops us werritin' about it all. We think it stops us wantin' and not wantin'. We doh stop though, do we?

Our Dave started workin' under the clock. None of us 'ad anythin' to do with 'im really. We day know 'im. I think our Tim led 'im along a bit. Rich still came in Turner's an' 'e was alright when 'e'd growd up. Rich'd said 'e'd sin Dave up in Horseley fields. 'E'd followed 'im into a corner shop and through some beaded curtains at the back.

"It wor no different from any other shop," Rich said. "Just on a row of High Street, sellin' the sem stuff as Sheena's. But there was a few men in theya. A few enterin' an' loiterin'. I went in, followed our Dave. I was

112

just gonna say 'ow do. Past the cans an' tins an' bread to the birr'at the back where the Sheenas an' Sids live. Through some bead curtain. I took one step in, it was dark an' it only 'ad a couple 'a light bulbs. All along the right side were sorta cubicles, like in the bogs. A long line of individual squares, built from cheap wood, plasterboard an' curtain poles. It fuckin' stank. Piss and shit and sweat and sex. Humid with it. It 'ad iss own mass it stunk that bad. Yo'd 'ear strange sounds. I took a slow step in and a quick step out again."

You'd 'ear Tim talk about sheddin' skins, not bein' afraid 'a change – that was part of it – removin' the past. Them days with Dave meant summat though, day they? They was both med from them days.

Tim

I didn't go to Dave's funeral, to be honest. That night at the truck stop when he was sobbin' and swearin', it stuck in my craw, like. I was angry. I didn't realise. He should've known what it all meant. To both of us, like.

It was Mick who told me. Funnily enough, like, we were at another funeral at the time. One of the Leathers. Thick George (don't ask). I was sat with him an' Nicki, an' Mick let it slip while people were still takin' their seats, like. I never told him too much. He'd have known we knew each other from school or Turner's an' whatnot.

"Yo' 'eard about Dave Firkins?"

I got through a pack of tissues for Thick George.

113

Joyce

Yvonne got comfortable and I did too. We were under the sheets. Warm, cosy.

"People at our school am the sem," she said. They ay worth bothering with. I hang around with the year elevens, but even they ay great."

We *got* it. Yvonne called it on the level, most people weren't. We got a bit deeper after the pikelets. She started talking about her parents.

"Mom works days an' Dad works nights so I only ever see 'em on a weekend," Yvonne never opened up, usually. "I have to get me own breakfast, an' sort out me babby sister. I walk 'er to school an' pick 'er up on my way 'ome. We 'ave tay together an' I'll leave Mom an' Dad's in the oven. Then 'er comes 'ome 'an 'e goos out. An' thass it, week in week out. They ay bad, them busy, they ay gorr'a choice in it. They doh see me. They doh look up to see 'ow iss gooin'. I used to gerrin' trouble at school an' the teachers said it was 'cause I was tryin' to get their attention. I thought they 'ad a point so I just stopped. They wor on the level so why should I try an' hoist 'em up?"

She let out her little cough-giggle, rolled her eyes and looked around the room. I tapped her on the knee.

"My sister's too young to know an' I ay gonna be a shit to 'er just 'cause Mom an' Dad cor be bothered. 'Er can come to Chicago wi' us when 'er's older. 'Er'll be alright with us, woh 'er? Anyway, it ay that bad. I still get to see you an' the gang an' Mom's always 'ome

114

before six so I 'ave me evenings. Everythin' else I'll do for myself, anyroad."

She had wide eyes as she spoke. Staring out to nowhere.

We smiled at each other. It was only the two of us.

"Everyone else can come and go." I told her. We smiled at each other and she hugged me. She kissed me on the cheek.

"Good night," she whispered.

I felt a sort of electric freeze shoot up my spine. My eyes widened. An ache started up in me. A throb. I couldn't sleep that night. Her thighs touched my waist. She'd laid in a way so she'd keep in touch with me. I kept leaning over to see if she was sleeping, I stared at her.

I didn't know what to do with this throb.

Michelle

It was 'er minge twitchin', wor it? Our Tim'd told me about Wyatt them years later. I knew that feelin'. Some of us gerr'it when weem kids. For no reason at all. I remember Gem used to do Ballet at the town hall an' there was summat about them girls gerrin' into their leotards that med me minge twitch. The bit in *The Lion, The Witch an' The Wardrobe* when the wolf gets stabbed, there was summat about that that med me minge twitch. I day realise what the twitch was, obviously, I was a kid. Then, when I was about eleven or twelve, it twitched when we was watchin' Bon Jovi on Dawn's Betamax, an' I knew then, day I? No one wants to remember these twitches 'cause it meks us all look queer.

I'd 'azzard a guess that this was when 'er changed. Like Nan said. I knew people like this, too. Shahid spent a summer wi' 'is elder cousins in Bradford one year 'an it took us all about two months to persuade 'im to stop pretendin' 'e was a tough northerner who day like the Sikhs an' day trust the Whites. "Yo' doh even goo to mosque, Shahid. Yo' said yo' 'ate it, so just come back an' fuck about wi' us again, yo' dick 'ead." Obviously, 'e 'ad to initiate into the gang again, day 'e?

Yvonne

It day tek much. I stopped at 'er's an' 'er mom med us tay. Doh get me wrong, I enjoyed meself. They was lovely an' Joyce was a top wench under it all. It day tek much though. I could see the way 'er looked at me. Wide eyed. I gid 'er a little hug, a little kiss, med 'er feel like it was only me an' 'er. I told 'er about Mom an' Dad an' I could tell 'er felt for me. It wor nothin'. Thass just 'ow it is. Burr'it 'elped with gerrin me in with 'er.

I started givin' 'er a little kiss when we went our ways. Like we was sisters. Like we was summat, anyroad. I know 'er loved that.

'Er legs was touchin' mine that night an' I day know what to mek 'a that.

Joyce

I didn't make much of the throb at the time. Just put it down to excitement. I had a friend, a best friend. We had a friendship that no one else had.

Mom and Dad took us to Stourton Lido once. We were on summer holiday. Me and Yvonne helped Mom with the picnic, she got us a bottle of pop each, said we could take them back to the shop when we were finished and get the shillings for glass. The lido was beautiful. You wouldn't think you were only a few miles out of Wolverhampton. It had a diving board and slide and there was decking all around the sides. We'd pretend we were in Capri. All of us did one way or another. Me and Yvonne had a great time – jumping in together, doing tandem down the slide – magic. I don't recall it properly, the feeling of it, I can only remember the feeling I got. There was something about Yvonne. Something special. She was tall and slim and beautiful. She looked older than she was. All the kids and all the dads kept looking at her in her swimming costume, slick against soft skin, shining in cool waters – something special. She had a way of making you look, everyone noticed her. She always stood out. She was mine, I loved that. They could look but no one else could have her.

We did all sorts of stuff that summer. Took our bikes down to Kinver and Highgate, spent hours lying together in the grasses, planning our American dream, climbed the big oaks. She started to squeeze my arm

117

when she got excited. We'd be talking and plotting and laughing and all that and then she'd reach over to me and touch my arm, give it a little squeeze. Every time, that throb came back.

Wherever we'd been and whatever we'd been doing, we'd part ways on a kiss. She'd lean in for a hug and peck me on the cheek. It wasn't anything really but she kissed me firmly, for a few seconds, I could feel her properly grip me when we hugged.

Our favourite thing to do was go to the cinema. We'd go once a week, at least. It helped with our plans. Yvonne would come over to Penn and we'd go to the pictures. A few weeks after *St Trinians* we went to see *Svengali*. It was bad. Yvonne said she read *Trilby* at school and that's what they based it on. It was bad but I remember wanting to have his control, to be able to play those mind games and win every time. I liked Svengali. He saw what he wanted and made it his.

When we got back to mine we did the same as last time. Mom made us pikelets and let us eat in bed. We chatted about school and family and all that stuff. She hadn't held me and she hadn't kissed me, but that throb came again. It came out of nowhere, from just being with her. I didn't think. I watched her sleep, imagining I was Svengali, transmitting my thoughts to her. I kissed her cheek. She was out cold. I kissed her lips. She stayed still and asleep. I don't know why, didn't know then and still don't, now, I was compelled. I'm not sure if it was all that sexual. I wanted to have her. I held a kiss on her. She didn't stir. I did it again and again. I wanted her to be mine, I wanted to consume her. I don't know how other people did it, don't know if they planned it. This just overcame me. I didn't think. Each time getting braver. Kissing for longer, kissing harder. Trying out neck, collar bone; breast. She made a little moan occasionally. She half made her half-cough-squeak. Juddered her limbs a little. I was terrified. I didn't think. But still, kept trying out my Svengali stare and returning my lips to her flesh. That was it. That's all that happened.

Bella

Time is different. Memory is difficult. Space – infinitesimal. You can't function when you're dead. Time slowed down when I was with her. Time was different. I felt an hour become ten when my tongue tasted her.

You get turned around in here. You turn, into and out from, in here. Coal seams still steam from bell pits, now brambled and birched over. The toddler tears of fireclay seep through the soils, where roots fossilise toil. Milk-stained fens hiccup out of almost-runs, built from feet daring to step over the edges.

In my time Roundoak thundered through on one side. The Pensnett train clatter-clacked its way throughout. Hingley and other small forges hissed and roared at the other end.

Now, I see it changed. It's difficult, but I see. Where the steelworks were, a shiny, bright and clean space –

an indoor town with plastic, tile and brass – you come and go like insects. From the remains of Roundoak, still warm before the rust, buds this hankersore – sharp, sanitised with slick polish. Instead of taming steel that feeds every chink of our space, you're sold stuff that breeds skulkworms over our loot. It chews and mottles larvae through our roots.

The forges, whimpering and dormant at Derby End. This, Saltwells, is a primordial belt-land, bridging the new and the ruined.

There are many of us who can't sleep in here. I am here. You call me Bella.

8

Michelle

Bella lingered over us. Bella an' the Wych-Elm. Like fleshy sewage washed up on a beach, it was a film that slicked over stuff.

Sometimes I think weem all so fucking predictable. Just goo to Turner's an' see us all. Old men bein' old men. Young wenches in tracksuits. We judge ourselves as 'arshly as you lot do. An' yo' ay no better. Like Grandad – 'e was tough an' 'e'd sin things but 'e'd sin enough to mek 'im not want to talk it through. 'E'd 'eard enough chat to mek 'im realise that talkin' day get nothin'. Like Carrick – 'e was tough an' 'e'd sin things, too. 'E'd tried 'ard to kip things together an' be a good mon but life 'ad just turned 'im the other way. Weem all the sem, ay we? Grandad ay never gonna tell us what went on in 'is life, even though he wants to share.   Gem ay never gonna stop bein' shy, even though 'er's beautiful an' everyone wants to be with 'er. Carrick'll buy you a drink an' ask 'ow you're doing but underneath there's still a part of 'im who blames you for 'is lot an' wants to knock it out 'a your yed. I doh know if iss our true self or what – but iss in us an' out 'a us, iss lurkin'.

You ay gonna get to the bottom of it.

Yvonne

The film was shit. Wuss than the book. That bloody Trilby an' 'er singin' an' 'er lovely feet. There was summat about that Svengali though. Yo' 'ad to be a little impressed, day ya?

It was lovely havin' tay cooked for us. I day 'ave to look after anyone, norr'even myself. They did it all. They day spare the butter. I 'ad that mix 'a comfy-guilt-control. Iss a sorta warmth.

But it was when I was startin' to fall asleep it 'appened. The dirty bitch. Fust it was alright – a goodnight kiss, like. But then 'er carried on; Neck, shoulder, arm . . . my tits. I was frozen. I still cor mek sense.

Iss abuse ay it? I dunno. I mean, I wor asleep. I coulda stopped 'er. But there was warmth to it an' 'er was gentle an' I'd bin kissed before but . . . I wanted to lamp 'er but I was froze an' I thought about that feelin' I'd mustered – that in-betweeny thing – warm an' cold an' angry an' calm an' I felt pinned down an' I felt like a hunter all at once. There was a throb about it. There's force in the passive too, ay there?

Carrick

"Alright our Dave," I said. I ant sin 'im since Tim fucked off. "'Ow am ya?"

"Alright Carrick," 'e said. "I'm okay, ta."

There wor no one down the fuckin' 'ope that night. Our Aisha was behind the bar. Big Lou sat nussin' a pint in the corner. Bob the Fish by the winda. Polish Pete an' 'is fuckin' racin' post. An' then us. 'E day look well. Like 'e'd bin on the fuckin' coke – skinny, sleepy.

"Pint, me mon?" I asked 'im.

"I'll get yo' one, Carrick."

"Yo' wo. Aisha, two more 'ere, bab."

I'd bin in since work got rained off. I'd med enough this fuckin' wik anyroad. Aisha 'anded over the pints, ticked me off a couple more on me tab.

"Whatcha know then, lad?" I asked 'im. I wor gonna ask.

"I've signed up for the army."

I choked a swig 'a me pint.

"Yo'? Fuckin' 'ell, Dave. Yo' gonna put a bit 'a fuckin' meat on ya fust?"

"Them Serbians ay much bigger."

Fuckin' fool. 'E ay never 'ad a scrap lerr'alone a fuckin' war. 'E can barely 'old isself up. I wanted to ask. I wor gonna ask.

"'Ave a goo at Polish Pete then," I said to 'im. "If them all fuckin' skinny like yo.'

'E laughed an' tried to shrug it off. I wor gonna ask.

"Maybe I could do with a bit 'a meat," 'E said.

I asked Aisha for a Jack. 'E took a big swig. 'E wanted out I think.

"Yo' in a rush?"

"I'm meetin' a mate in a bit."

Meetin' a dealer, more like. Fuckin' eejit. 'E was part of it. 'E looked at me. We was both quiet. I downed me Jack. 'E took a swig an' 'e 'ad 'is eye on me. 'E fuckin' knew summat. I looked back. Slammed the glass down and turned towards 'im. 'E sorta blinked or winked an' looked at me then away. 'E fuckin' knew. I day 'ave to ask.

Stan walked in.

"Alright Carrick, yo' paddy bastard?"

"On ya way then, lad," I said to Dave, raised me 'ond to Stan.

"'Ow do Stan, yo' old cunt."

Joyce

I barely slept. I spent the whole night tossing and turning – terrified that she'd felt all those kisses and that she'd been too freaked out to stop me or do anything. She'd just laid still and waited for it to be over and as soon as she could, she'd fuck me up. I lay awake most of the night with that empty stomach feeling. I lay awake with flushes of heat in my face, shivers in my limbs. I tried to make plans on how to discredit her. I tried to think of ways of getting out of school, out of the area, out of the country. I tried to figure out how to be alone. I tried to think about what kissing my best friend meant. Mom and Dad were lovely, they'd do anything for me, but this? I had to figure it out.

Mom always said I liked things clean. I always wanted stuff in its right place. I always reacted well to it. That's been something else I've been trying to work on. I'm sorry. It's not always as simple as I thought. Not always as easy to file things as I always tried. I'm sorry.

When she woke she smiled. Said she'd had horrible dreams about that awful film. She laughed at herself. She was lovely as ever. We had breakfast with my parents and they dropped her home. She was the same. I was the same. I just pretended that nothing had happened, if she hadn't realised then that was fine, we'd just carry on being the same mates we'd always been. I'd shake off the feeling and it wouldn't happen again. It was *Svengali*. Just the idea of it. Just the film.

We'd said we'd meet after Church on Sunday. Meet down on Cinder Bank and go have a look at the boat show on the Bumble Hole Canal Basin. They still have it there too, down on the canal at Bumble Hole – loads of barges, all painted up with lovely colours – roses, castles, strange names and those funny jars they use as vases.

So we met where Cinder Bank meets Halesowen Road. Yvonne had to look after her sister in the morning so I walked from the bus stop on my own. We hugged, as usual. But she didn't grip me. Sort of held onto my elbows and tensed.

It was a lovely day. One of those amazing spring days – bright and blue and lush. The smell of candyfloss and the musk of seeds. All the colours and boats. They had craft stalls and a band, playing fiddles and squeezeboxes. We went on a boat tour through the Dudley Tunnel. It's pitch black in there. They had a couple of volunteers to do the leggin'. Yvonne let me take her hand but, well, I held the back of her hand. A limp hand. It should've been a really great day.

I kept getting that empty stomach feeling. Sweats and shivers. She knew. Maybe they all knew. But what could I do? I couldn't very well ask her what was wrong. I couldn't ask why she didn't want to come to mine. I couldn't stop hanging out with her either. I couldn't get enough of her. It was still just me and her, in a way. I couldn't stop hanging out with her.

That shivering. That empty stomach. It came back those years later with Tim. I didn't know how to tell him. I'd spent too long being closed up and learning to like it.

I asked her back to mine a few times more.

"Friday night pictures?" I asked.

"I can't."

I remember when my uncle got divorced. They'd only been together for a year. My Dad took him for a pint and

Like standin' on the edge of a cliff, fightin' the urge to jump, 'avin' to goo back an' do it again and again. It ay as simple as good against bad, nice against nasty, gain against loss – iss like an oil that slicks between two poles.

Shahid

Ages agoo, Sam and Jay throwd mah shoe in the cut. *Fuckin' kaminas. Fuckin' lolas.* Ah'd bin showin' off about this new pair Bibi 'ad got me, so Jay pinned me down an' Sam took off mah shoe and threw it off the bridge. Ah went ape. *Ma Chid.* Ah shouted at 'em. *Kutti Ka Bacha*, Ah called 'em. Ah jumped in to gerr'it, but ah was poor an' ant bin to the baths an' day 'av no muscle back then so ah was just like a tadpole stuck in a puddle, flippin' about an' wrestlin' for life. Ammi would've killed me if ah'd lost 'em. *Fuckin' Kaminas. Fuckin' lolas.* Ah was shit at swimming, ya know. Every time ah got in the water ah was gonna die, ah'd flap abart but it was all panic. Proper panic, man. But ah 'ad to, me Bibi 'ad spent loads on them shoes 'an Dad always said we was skint. Ah still get light headed an' lose me breath when we ay got nothin' in the cupboard. Ah 'ad to dive down. 'Ad mah eyes closed and was ferritin' about to try an' grab 'em. Ah got to a point when Ah 'ad to breathe, Ah 'ad to come up for air. Not like on the cross country or whatever, when y'um out of breath, this was proper – if Ah doh breath right now Ah'll die. But at the sem time Ah couln't

129

leave the water. Ah 'ad to keep tryin'. *Aage kuan peeche khaee*, we say, in-between the devil and the sea. An' thass when it builds. You try an' ignore it an' that meks it wuss. You keep tryin' an' that meks it wuss. It just builds an' builds until it busts. Ah day drown. Ah day get mah shoe either. Sam an' Jay 'ad to get theya moms to cough up. *Fuckin' Kaminas.*

Thass wharr'iss like though, ay it? You doh know what to do for the best an' you get stuck between places – an' thass when it builds.

Like that *Buri Nazar* in the woods. Down in that openin' where all the greens and grasses turn to shit. That tree. Ah cor even remember really. But it builds. Ah got stuck. It was them that dared me again, *gaand ka bukhaar*, we say, pain in the ass. Jay said to follow the path through the bell pits, past the quarry an' then ya cut up through the brackens. It gets dark. It gets quiet. Ah wo' goo back.

It wor anything to start with. The tree's massive an' it teks the whole of that space up. Iss odd. It smells – evil eye – *Buri Nazar*. Then when yo' notice the smell, yo' notice yo' legs – they ay stiff but they wo' work. Yo'm stuck. Thass when it builds. Thass when yo'm stuck – inbetween – festerin'. An' there's summat there. Watchin'. Ah don't know what Ah saw, maybe nothin', but summat was theya.

"Teri gand ma keera hai," Ah shouted out. "An insect in yo' ass." Then Ah fell.

Bella

It's a constant throb – but miniscule like a whimper from behind a deep breath. It starts from where I am and leaks out slowly, meandering about the woods to the bypass that announces the edge of town. It's like metal sawing against metal. It's a game of Chinese whispers. It's a series of ticks and whistles that swirl.

There was once a track the odd rambler would stumble across. The track can no longer be traced.

There is a little patch of land, overgrown with bushes, brambles and weeds. A small opening of wet soil. I let the thicket grow. It camouflages, creeps and engulfs. It has buried us here beautifully. Small insects and rodents gather in the green and brown to build their nests.

Many saunter straight past without notice. They have done for years. It's quiet and desolate. Nature creeps. At night large animals pass by and sniff around for things to steal. Foxes, stoats and badgers reel around. I'm out of the way as they sweep. There's no intimacy. Just an exchange. That is nature.

The whisper of rumours calls a few out.

I look down on the road where cars zip by and the people sprint about. The jigsaw patterns of developments – their pristine shine. I see the glass and metal, choking and raging. I'm among the great history. I mark moment to moment. And I send out little whispers. I own nothing. All of my movements are in autumn. I sit in my thicket away from it all. I am being.

Curious people, lost in the dark or people who have

come to see for themselves if the rumours are true, they see little. They run away. Tripping, breaking away little by little.

It is a hard lesson, being alone. I still go down to the edge of the woods for a peek. The rumours work. A little sign here and there. Each tale needs a flint.

She led me along the old track. I still had cravings. It could have been anyone, but she was easy, kind, trusting – easy.

When the rumours started, people made up such fables.

There were the two of us around. The tree too distant to see or hear. All of those fables. I work hard and I stay invisible. I am being.

They were the first for some time, those boys. It was dusk and the sky flamed pink and orange. They were tempted and afraid and shamed. Like I was. Like all of us. I had to do it, to view it.

No one came to find me, deep down in the Wych-Elm. They know that it's just a story and that the woods are dense and full of those whispers. You can easily lose your way back from here. You can easily lose your way.

sausage rolls. Our Trace's boyfriend set up his radio in the corner. They had a sort of DIY skittles lane and we sat around the edges as the little ones clattered balls, thunderous and constant.

I sat with Dad all night, just the two of us. They tried to talk to me. The cousins wanted me to dance and play. They tried. I just grunted at them. For the rest of the night they kept their distance. They stayed on their side of the hall.

"What is with you, Joyce?" Dad asked. "First school, now this. You're making a show of yourself."

I gave him a smirk. He gave me a look.

Uncle Flow came over. He was everyone's plumber, not a real uncle.

"Why ay ya muckin' around wi' the others, bab?" He asked me. "Looks like fun to me. Goo on, me wench. Let me an' yo' old mon 'ave a chat."

"My old man doesn't want to talk to your sort," I said. "I don't want to play with them, either." Arms folded. Cute Yvonne-type smile and eyebrow-raise.

Driving home, Dad spoke to Mom like I wasn't there.

"We've got to do something about Joyce, love." Dad said. "It's gone too far. I think we made a mistake. We didn't let her find her way, make her choice. We've made a mistake with her. We've got to do something, love."

Mom looked back through the rear view mirror, rested a hand on Dad's knee.

"It's just a teenage thing, isn't it, love?"

"Maybe," Dad said.

Maybe. It clings to everything, that word.

Sid

I went back to the woods to look for it. Your granddad said, Y'om mad, Sid. I said doh look for 'er, day I?

I told 'im I 'ad to, I was scared. Like Bella 'ad passed summat on to me. Said it was a Qarin. Sheena called it evil eye – *Buri Nazar*. We all 'ave one. Summat that whispers to you. Meks you do stuff. Thought that warr'ever was out in Saltwells was a Qarin. They attach themselves to people, places. I thought it was attached to Shahid and Sheena, all of us. Each one of us has his own Qarin. They try to turn you against Allah.

So I went back to Saltwells an' back to the Wych-Elm. Stayed theya all night, sat by the tree, praying. Nothin' 'appened. It was a bit bloody weird, yeah, but there wasn't anything like bloody last time, yeah, just dark and lonely and bloody cold. Nothin' 'appened until I got up to leave. It was almost mornin' so I could start to see all the shadows of the woods a bit clearer. I got up and started to walk off but summat med me turn around.

I'd been bloody sat there all bloody night, and nothing had happened. It was dark and cold and your eyes play tricks on you, but that was all. Nothing bloody happened. But when it was almost light, when I could just start to make out things and I got up to go – bloody hell! Something bloody made me turn around.

138

I'd sat there all night praying – *'A 'oothu billaahi minash-Shaytaanir-rajeem* – in the dark, I was frightened, but I prayed – *Allaahummak-fineehim bimaa shi'ta.* Just when it was almost safe, when it was almost light and I was walking out, something made me turn around. And there she was – Qarin. Filthy clothes, cuts on her skin. Pale. Skinny. Dark eyes. Evil eyes. She bloody stared without blinking. Straight bloody through me. I only looked at her for a second. I've never ran so bloody fast.

Michelle

There'd bin loads 'a stories like this. We wor allowed in Saltwells. Not many people did goo in. There'd always be one or two down Turner's who'd tell a tale. We'd laugh when they told 'em. Then try an' shake it out 'a our sleep later.

Stan

Our Michelle doh remember, does 'er? 'Er's obsessed though, ay 'er. 'Er'll probably get to the truth one day. Cross me heart she doh. 'Er 'ad nightmares for the fust year after it 'appened, 'er did. Me an' 'er nan took it in turns to calm 'er down. 'Er an' Gem shared a room when we moved to Sledmere an' that sorted 'em out. 'Er'd wek up in sweats an' shiverin, 'er would. 'Er'd be iverrin' and werritin' an' 'er'd say some weird stuff when 'er was wakin' but not awake.

The trees can watch you! They can. They sid us! They did.

Me an' 'er nan do our best, we do. 'Er's turned out well really, 'er 'as. Weem proud of 'er. An' our Gem. Like I says, 'er doh remember but summats stuck, ay it. Summats stuck to 'er, it is.

Joyce

I got grounded for talking to Uncle Flow like I did. Not that it mattered.

I couldn't shake it. Those dreams of being caught, found out, that strange looking woman in the dirty clothes. I can't shake those dreams of Saltwells now, either. I was on my own. I didn't go out. The gang would all be gossiping about it. Mom and Dad were worried.

"I do think we need to listen to some experts on this, don't you?" Mom said.

"I think we know what's best. Not people who haven't been around," Dad said.

"That's as maybe, but it can't hurt can it? We can try it. We could take her to see someone. Do you think – the girls' school – you and her doing boys' things together . . . ?"

"Boys things? I don't accept that."

"So we just ignore what's happened then?"

"We don't ignore it. We just don't get over-excited by it."

"It's our Joyce we're talking about."

"I know it's our Joyce. You don't think I know?"

It was never overly obvious, the arguing, the *our Joyce* of it all, but that sort of thing sinks deeper, doesn't it?

Mom had gone to see Auntie and the Cousins. She'd gone to take flowers over. Uncle Flow wasn't even a real uncle. It wasn't that much really. I wasn't nasty, just not nice. Mom had it in her head they'd taken offense. They were different from us, Mom and Dad had moved to Penn when he got bumped up to being a manager, we had an indoor toilet and we'd been to France and Spain. I don't think it bothered them but Mom was always cautious with manners, especially with them.

I shut myself away in my room and Dad sat in his chair. It was when she came back it all went up.

At first it was just raised voices and I tried not to be bothered. I just sat in my room. But their voices went on longer than normal. They were louder. I couldn't pretend. I slipped out of my room and crawled along the landing to the top of the stairs. Just lay there listening. They were in the living room and they'd have to come out and come back on themselves on the stairs before they saw me. I'd hear them coming. "Well, how do we know they're not making it up?" Dad said.

"I suppose we don't, but come on, it adds up, doesn't it?"

". . . I suppose. Let's not get carried away though, eh? Maybe we need to look into things a bit first."

"That's just like you, fathers and their daughters, she can never do wrong, can she?"

141

I'd stopped breathing. Every muscle tensed up.

"We need to check it out. Make sure all the details add up. I mean do you really trust the word of your sister's kids? Do you really trust your sister?"

I'll never forget this talk. Never forget these words. I was frozen. I just lay there listening to it all unfold. I bit my knuckle, I didn't blink. I was frozen – just a corpse on the landing. Their conversation continued.

"I do trust her, yes," Mom said. "Maybe not all of it, but . . . "

"No smoke without fire? That's what you're saying."

"Maybe."

"That's charming."

"It's our Joyce! I'm worried!"

"Alright!"

"Don't alright me again, and don't play the *my sister's kids* card again. Joyce never had friends. She had you. Then she had Yvonne. And she lost you."

"She didn't lose me."

"Really?" Mom paused. "It's been three weeks since they've been out together and now we get all of this mess."

"So, what do you want to do? Take her up the clinic?"

"*I* think, and think this through first, love, think it properly, think it with the dad-hat taken off for a second; that we need to speak to Yvonne."

All the blood rushed to my head. My stomach emptied. Every inch of me was in spasm.

"Yvonne?"

"I don't feel there's any other way to get to the bottom of what's troubling our Joyce."

Bella

It's not just the memory. Not just time and space. It's the not-now of it all. It's never now anymore. When I watch you, you're in a present I can never be part of, and I still can't get back to mine. So when I watch you, walking your dog, kissing your girlfriends, playing hide and seek, I see you watching me back. Every time you step into these woods you watch me back. You might not even know it. You can't avoid it. Sometimes, it'll creep up on you. It'll stop you in your tracks for a split second, like something caught in the corner of your eye. It's me. I'm looking back at you to see you looking back at me.

She made me think of that song when she led me through the woods. We left the pub, not together, but at the same time. We were both looking back to see if the other was looking back to see. This runs over and over, here, stuck in these woods – stuck in this nether. It plays on repeat.

We forget the cold, the damp, the dirt. We fight it off with nibbles on the neck, with sucking nipples, with tender tickles over skin. We become warm, flushed. We forget everything in fucking. We become only heartbeats. We are panting, curious and starving. We're tranced in each kiss, each flex and stroke. Tranced in the shiver of it – the shiver that pins and needles its way up in waves. Waves break. Spread out. Stretch.

It plays on repeat.   Memory is difficult.   We see ourselves looking in and out. Looking forward and back. It plays on repeat. Waves break.

It was the crack of a twig that made her turn. I froze. And then we heard the footsteps.   We heard the whispered mutter. We stopped. We froze. Whispers and footsteps closed in.

I still can't see what direction. You seem to envelope us. Imprisoned.

10

Michelle

Gem 'ad a mate who worked in Bushy Fields Mental 'Ospital – fuckin' 'orrible place. 'Er told 'orrid stories about them lot, shittin' 'emselfs, cuttin' up theya arms, mekin' 'emselfs sick an' stuff. 'Er said it was always cold an' it always stank: 'a sanitiser, sick an' shit. It was grey an' pale green. The colour 'a the wench in *The Exorcist*. No wonder no one got well. These places 'ave changed, but they need to change more too, I reckon. Weem all different now an' weem all in our own 'eads all the time. There ay nothin' real an' we cor find ourself so iss all gorr'a be different, 'cause we could all end up theya pretty easily, an' most of us 'ave got somethin' gooin' for us in that way. One 'a the things with them though is they 'ave a sort 'a contagious thing about them. There's a weight about Bushy

145

Fields, a gravity. Like when we talk about the Wych-Elm and the woods, what keeps you out is the sem as what pulls you in.

I needed to find out. Bella infiltrates us. She slicks into our pores. All these tales do. The fossils in Wrens Nest, the ruins 'a the steel shafts, the sink 'oles, Stambermill Viaduct, the stories – them all part 'a us. All this mix 'a history and folktale. Thass where weem from. Thass who we am. It all comes down to this. I live on the sem rode as the Tipton Slasher did, weem med 'a tough stuff 'ere. It all seeps into us. Iss natural for us to be creative, 'ere. We built our world turning sand into crystal so iss in our blood – alchemy is. Even the beer. We build ourselves up on all sorts. Even the beer gets treated. See the Batham's Brewery 'as iss own well, so the water they use in the brew comes through the coal seam, doh it. Thass why you get that taste. It cor be replicated.

Bella infiltrates us. 'Er's under our streets, under our feet. 'Er was right around the corner all the time.

One 'a the old timers in Ma' Pardoe's used to love Bella stories. 'E'd written local history books. No one knew 'ow old 'e was. Not many people liked 'im 'cause 'e went on a bit an' 'e always looked like 'e'd bin dredgin' the cut with 'is fingers. Anyroad, 'e said that when 'e was a lad, 'is dad owned a factory in Quarry bank an' 'e did the last shift on a Fridee when 'e was a bab. 'E used to walk 'ome through Saltwells. One night 'e 'eard a woman screamin'.

"It was always quiet in them woods," 'e said. "But

this scream, it wor like nothin' I'd 'eard before, it was like a sow. There was a wench called Joan who worked in the butchers who was a little way up the path too, an' 'er froze, so I think to meself, it cor just be in me yed. So me an' Joan set abart lookin' but we day see a thing. Them screams echoed through Saltwells. Bounced off all the bonks and trees so we day know from wheya they was comin'. We give up after a bit an' told the police, like. Thass as close as anyone got to Bella. They day find 'er for two years an' no one else 'eard them screams 'cept for me and Joan. Joan was lovely wench ... "

'E was alright, that old 'un. Bit of a blether yed, thass all.

Joyce

I almost screamed. As soon as that name was mentioned, I choked down a scream. *Yvonne.* All the tight muscle fear just snapped. I was stiff. A lump swelled in my throat. I focused on the floral wallpaper – the endless fractal repetitions. Slowly got to my feet and tip-toed back to my room.

I packed my bag while they slept. A couple of weeks-worth of clothes and underwear, some soap and toothpaste and whatnot. It was late, well past midnight. *Get out. Start again.* I was clear. No finite plan but my mind was cool, steady. I jumped the gap from my window to the porch. Landed on the narrow roof and climbed down holding onto the railing. I started walking in the pitch black, not thinking. Not daydreaming, really, just staring, in half-thought. My stride was wide. My breath was deep. Watching the sleepy suburbs of Penn, with its tree lined streets and semi-detached homes, become Himley, with their hectares of neatly cropped fields, hay bales, manure, that great looming house. Over the odd bits of wild meadow and greens stuck between terraces and old barns, then hitting Gornal. Then Dudley, cutting past the top church and through the zigzag of red bricks. It was early, the morning moon lingered, cutting through grey mists and wisps of cloud. Netherton loomed. Yvonne.

I knew why I was there. Yvonne.

I'd kissed Yvonne. It's something else if you say it out loud, though. I didn't have the guts. It was different back then. I couldn't get the measure of myself. I couldn't say it out loud and make it real.

Tim

I'd been imprisoned in my own way, like, by the lampin', the rumours an' all that. Most of what happened to me had a bit of choice in it, to be honest I hadn't done nothin' wrong, as such like, but I made myself strange.

I never said I was gay, but I said enough to make whatever I am a thing, like, an identity, an' I lived with that even though some folks couldn't, like. I med myself what I wanted.

Honestly, we all wanna be different an' the same, doh we? Weem from Netherton – it ay Cradely, it ay

Dudley, an' we're different from one side of the bonk to the other, like, but they're in the Black Country too so if it's a choice between all of us an' Brum then we're the sem again, like. Then if some bloke from London gets involved then Brum gets in on it too an' we become West Midlands, like, then if the Frogs come we're England. An' all the time there's a bit of us that's just us, that no one can touch, it's just ours, like. We think. We're all the sem an' different. We all mek it in ourselves and for others. It ay real. But it stains.

Michelle

Carrick'd said 'e day feel imprisoned until the fust night. 'E said it day sink in 'til the screws turned the lights off.

"Thass when you know yo'm on your fuckin' own," Carrick said. "Thass when yo' know you gorr'a wake up and fuckin' face it."

Grandad said the sem about bein' in the forces. 'E was out in Malaya after the war. 'E said it felt like a scout camp until that fust night in the jungle.

"Yo' doh know dark until yo'm in the jungle at night, me wench."

If you ay got reasons you cor mek sense, if you cor mek sense it festers. Thass why Carrick was like 'e was. Thass why Sid 'ad to goo back to the woods. Thass why we all 'ad to figure out these stories about Bella. I needed to know. Things fester and festering spreads. Just look at the tomatoes up in Quarry Bank. We'd built concrete on concrete. Factories on factories. Estates

149

on top 'a estates. Never reckoning the bitch 'a nature lurkin' under it all, mullin', rottin', renewin'. Weem a strange mix 'a green an' grey, 'ere. Weem a strange mix 'a old an' new, death an' birth, real an' unreal. Weem like algae growin' on a pool 'a rust stained water.

Who put Bella in the Wych-Elm?

Joyce

The throb came upon me. The throbbing and I felt sick.

They'd all be down Saltwells, circled around Yvonne as she told them about how Joyce Wyatt was a disgusting dike and how they'd sent her to hospital. They'd laugh and tell jokes and pass it on to my cousins, and then everyone would know. That's how it happened. Maybe Yvonne just let it slip or someone guessed and she didn't deny it. Whatever. It spread like chicken pox. The quick disintegration of our friendship, my school work and all that, and now.

I bit my knuckle and it bruised. Steadied myself.

I hadn't thought it through. I'd kissed her and I felt strange. I wanted to consume her, make her mine. That empty stomach feeling again. I bit my knuckle and it pierced the skin. But that wasn't all.

Mick

Down the 'ope, thass where they was. Talkin' about our Tim. An' one on 'em, 'er was a bloody specials nurse. For the mongs. 'Er stook 'er penneth in, day 'er. Called 'em behaviours!

150

Fuckin' behaviours! Fuckin' judgement call! Dirty little bastards! Think they can control it all, doh they. Shit! One 'a these days there's gonna be a queue at the courts with a ton 'a trannies suin' them cunts.

Tek 'em to court! All the others should an all! They ay god an' they think iss all simple. It ay. Some men am proper men, an' some am different, an' weem all strange an' weem all always changin'. An' in the guts of us all we all know weem messy. It ay simple an' I doh think there's just boys and girls anyroad. I mean, weem born with tons a stuff in us, genes an' chromosomes an' all sorts. Yo' have a look in a science book an' see what a stew 'a stuff humanity is med of – an' they try an' tell us iss all down to two chromosomes, come on. But that one decision, it fucks all sorts up – it fucks families, friends, schools. It fucked up generations.

Like our Nicki says, call it what it is – potty trainin'. They treat yo' like a babby, t'ay nothin' more than sittin' on the naughty step. Thass right.

Bella

Memory is difficult but I remember feelings, smells. I think I do.

In the springtime the woods are fresh, green, wet. They are acrid, fetid. We're stuck in the muck of it all.

We were all over each other. We couldn't let each other go. Her lips, tongue, teeth against my neck, my breast. Hot breath. Panting. She pinned my arms behind my back. Face pressed into my frame. Ripped back my skirt.

151

Circled cunt.

Memory is difficult. It's just flashes of moods.

This is when you came. We heard the snap of twigs, the muttering voices, the muted footsteps. This is when we froze. We stopped. Stared at each other, scared. You were ten strong against us. You stepped through the thicket and out into our space. Circled us.

Joyce

Cinder Bank is a criss-cross of redbrick terraces. A maze of little family homes all connected, running into each other. There's a line, framed by walls that run the length of the streets, separating the yards of one road and the other. There's a line, a path that cuts between two rows. That's where I went.

"Yvonne," I whispered. It was dusky. It was quiet. Just a little breeze and the odd alley cat. "Yvonne."

I held my breath. Listened. Nothing. Just the little breeze. Just the odd alley cat.

I picked up a pebble and launched it at the window, I held my breath. Listened. Nothing. Repeat. Bigger pebble. Launch. That's when the silence broke. It happened quickly. Smash. The pebble went straight through the window. It shattered – a clank-clatter-crash.

"The fuck?" a voice screamed. Then a light came on. Then a face at the broken frame.

"What the fuck am yo' doin', Joyce?"

"We need to talk."

"Yo' need to gerr'outta 'ear. My old mon's 'ome in a bit."

"Yvonne, we were best friends. Come on . . . "

"That was before yo' become a perv, Joyce. Now get lost."

"You don't mean that, just . . . "

"Doh tell me what I mean, Joyce. Yo' crossed a line."

I fell silent. Sighed. Just stared up at 'er.

"You took advantage of us," I said. "You played on how nice my mom and dad are."

"I ay gerr'in to who took advantage, Joyce. I was willin' to kip it to myself. I doh want the taint. I doh want the 'assle. It was always a game, yo' blether-yed. I played yo'. Just leave."

I just stared up at her. Let out a long breath. "Yvonne!"

"Wass gooin' on?" A man's voice. I turned. Yvonne's neighbour had come through his back gate.

"Er's crazy, Niall, broke the bloody winda wi a bibble, ay 'er."

He turned to me. "There's a babby in theya. Who d'ya think yo' am?"

He stepped forward into the gulley and I turned to run. But he was quick for an old chap and he held onto my arm. "Yo' ay gooin' nowhere, bab."

I swung my arm at him and caught him on the cheek. Saw his eyes widen in the dark. In a second he had my arm pulled up behind my back and my face into the tarmac. I couldn't keep it in. I screamed. My heart thumped. Face burned. Limbs shivered. Gums sore with teeth clenched. Spittle. Sweat. Tears. My tongue tasted salt, metallic.

"Get off," I shouted. "I'm only a girl."

"Yo'm a bloody vandal an' a thug, me wench."

Inhale. Exhale. Inhale. My heart ran thump-thump tha-rump. I was hot and shivering, every inch tensed.

"Snap 'er arm," Yvonne called. "Snap 'er bloody arm."

"Go up to Bill's, Yvonne," he said. "'E'll tek 'er in."

Bill lived at number two. He was the local bobby. Niall held me down as we waited.

"I doh get beat, Joyce." Yvonne whispered as I was carried off. "Yo'm beat. I doh wanna 'ear from yo'. Doh wanna see yo' again. I doh get beat."

That's the last we spoke.

Dave

"Hand it over," They said. They 'ad me pinned to the wall 'a the boys'. Gripped me blazer an' pushed me against the lockers. "Hand it over, faggot."

I've 'ad 'eadache for days an' I ay slept. *I dipped me 'ond in me pocket an' pulled out the quid Mom 'ad given me for lunch, 'onded it over. I was tiny. I was always small, still am. There was three on 'em. Year nines. One on each side wi' a grip on me. One in the middle pokin' finger in me face.* I need money, an' these shivers. Fuck. There's sores all over – blisterin'.

"An' the watch," the middle 'un said. "I'll 'ave the watch an' all."

I shook me yed. It was a Swatch Dad'd given me last birthday. I shook me yed. I'm shekkin' now an' I cor stop scratchin' an' the sweat wears me. Tomo should come around soon. 'E'll be 'ere today. Get some crank. Get some levellers.

"No ay an' answer 'ere, Dave, yo' queer." 'E grabbed me wrist an' undid the watch. Slipped it away from me wrist. "Come on, lads," 'e said to the others. Then they turned to leave.

It was the fust time I'd met 'im. I day know then what 'e'd become. What 'e'd do to me. Every time I move me lips they crack. Me joints am tight – seized up. *I'd sid 'im about an' I knew everyone called 'im Brolley. Yo' couln't miss 'im, 'e day care 'ow much 'e stood out.*

They turned an' stood in the doorway.

"Yo' gorr'a problem, mate?"

"I ay yer mate," 'e said. Shrugged and grinned. "Give 'is watch back."

"Or what?" The middle 'un said.

"Give 'is watch back." 'E took a step forward, towards 'em.

There was three on 'em. One took a step back. Tim day tek 'is eyes off 'em. It was like a Van Damme film. Thass 'ow I feel – like the bloke at the end 'a *Kickboxer* – like when Van Damme crossed the desert in *Awol*.

Then the lad who stepped back spoke.

"Tim Carmody, ay it?"

"Thass right," Tim said. "CARM-O-DY!"

The middle lad dropped the watch to the floor. Tim stepped to the side an' the lads walked through. 'E

jerked 'is yed out as the middle lad past 'im. The dick
flinched an' skipped off.

Tim walked over to me. I was shekkin'. I'm shekkin.
Me nose kips bleedin'. These blisters am weepin'. I'm
shekkin. That Tomo's forgot ay 'e? Probably just lookin'
afer isself. Tim put 'is 'ond on me shoulder. Gid it a rub.
I looked up arr'im – them big brown eyes.

"Come on," 'e said. "Come an' meet me mate, Rich."

I smiled an' walked wi' 'im. I was mates wi' a
Carmody. 'E split is lunch wi' me that day – corned beef
an' brown sauce.

Bella

Memory is difficult. It's hard but I still sense parts. Light
breezes. The night-time outline 'a bushes and branches.
Rustles. Her breath on my neck. Circling fingers over
my frame. Then the footsteps. Then you stepping out
from the thickets to face us. Then dread. Then enclosure.
Then you closing in.

She'd stripped me. Goose-pimpled skin stuck to the
bark 'a the Wych-Elm. It was just us two. Then you –
surrounding, closing in. Dread. Throb. Thump. How
could we even scream? We putrefy like this old trunk.
We're hounded.

I am still here. Guardian. Prisoner. Portent. You call
me Bella.

11

Michelle

Tell me about your father. That was my first reaction when Tim told me about Wyatt an' 'er dad.

It was so saft. So obvious. I doh think Freud ever said that, iss like everyone gerrin the Casablanca line wrong, ay it? *Play it again, Sigmund.* We did A-Level Freud at Halesowen College, I thought 'e was a perv. An' a bit of a blether-yed an' all. Iss all eyes an' cocks, ay it?

Gem always said, "'e day understand nothin', just med up a bunch 'a stuff. Put 'is own daddy and arse issues on us all. I doh know any wench who wanted a cock, an' if they did it wor 'cause they thought they'd lost theyas. If men knew the clit they'd want the clit."

Er 'ad a point, day 'er?

*'Ow many Freudians does it take to screw in a penis
... eh, lightbulb?*

Joyce

"I knew your mother just after the war," the desk
sergeant said. "Top wench. Looked after my leg." He
tapped the stump below his knee. He saw Dad's leg
too, and he knew.

Dad paid for a new window and it turned out Uncle
Flow could sort a few other things out for them too –
he'd worked with Yvonne's dad on a couple of sites a few
years back. The three of them and a couple of policemen
spoke in the office as the desk sergeant took a damp
cloth to my face.

"You're grounded," Dad said, driving home.

I shrugged.

"Shrugging? You think that'll help you, do you?
That's part of the issue, I think, Joyce. You're spoilt."

I shrugged again. Gave him an Yvonne smile. He
went quiet for a while. Dudley became Sedgley, and
we pulled through Penn Common. It was light now.
Early birds were walking their dogs through the wispy
grass. Somewhere between gold and green it waved, an
endless-wriggling-conjoined-serpent.

"You never had any brothers or sisters, Joyce,"

I looked up at him.

"Just let me say this."

He checked his mirrors. Pulled over.

158

"Me and your mom couldn't have any more kids. We were lucky to have you. Maybe we took it too far. Maybe I tried to be a dad and a brother and a mate. Maybe Mom was too keen on the girls' school. We did our best, Joyce."

"I'm sorry, Dad."

"I'm not going to tell your mom the full story. She already thinks too much about the Yvonne situation."

"What?" My neck jerked back towards the common and the waves of long grass. He went quiet again.

"You don't really have friends do you, Joyce? Maybe it's going out like a boy scout with me. I won't go as far as to say you feel . . . but it is . . . ? Something's become clouded. Do you agree, Joyce?"

"What do you mean, Dad? Where's this coming from?"

"There's clearly something. That's what I mean. You can't go around breaking windows just because Yvonne doesn't . . . and there's the legal issue too. Do you understand, Joyce?"

"I don't understand."

"You're grounded. You're lucky, too."

Bella

You call me Bella but you had no name for me back then. Back there in the cool woods I was alien.

I can't count you. You may have been three strong or ten. I remember rope and I remember the splintered leg of a table. Dread. You close in – cane handed.

She slipped her grip from me. Turned. Sprinted. I still see her, slight and swift. She scuppered past your mob and skulked away through the woods. Sick. Dread. Left. I was dropped.

Tim

To be honest, with Dave and Dad, and the guys back at school, you learn pretty quickly how to cover things up, like. You get good at it. But it sits within you. It sits like a worm, gnawing. With Dave I had to get away, like, with all of 'em really, I had to cut ties. Like Wyatt, you have to learn to stay undercover, like, doesn't matter who takes the hard end for the sake of the cover up, as long as it isn't you. Honestly, that's hard, isn't it?

With Mom and Dad I 'ad to be a good son, like, a good Catholic son, a proper mon, too. You know my old mon, honestly, better to fake it. Thass it though, ay it? Iss the fakin', the lurkin' about with life that stuff spreads an' festers.

I was drunk an' no one had bothered to come down to the truck stop that night, they'd already called last orders, like. I was in a state an', honestly, it was one of them nights when you need some thrill or some company. I started walkin' up to Cradley Cemetery. Dave was from Netherton but it was Cradley Road end. I didn't have a clue where he was buried, like, and I didn't have enough sense or light to start lookin'. I just got to the gates. They were locked. I gave them a kickin'. Tried to climb them. Bruised all my back an'

160

arse. An' I had a cry and I said sorry and I said thanks.

Honestly, I find myself there in dreams sometimes. I can sometimes taste stuff in my dreams, like. They sorta give me that backa the mouth, smelly taste.

Joyce

Dad could be thanked.

I knew the rules. There's a blueprint to family, friends, school. You can follow it. You can manipulate it too, I did. I suppose I've done it a lot – all my life. It's hard to change. I'm sorry.

I stopped going out with Dad, bird watching and picking damsons. Things with Mom were fine. She was quiet. Dad kept a keen eye on me. I was grounded, indefinitely.

"We'll see some improvement at school first, Joyce. Then maybe you can go and see your cousins."

We had a walk and a bag of chips on a Friday, me and Dad. We had 'chats'. I was straight back to school. No respite. It was fun lying about it all, it made me look cool in some ways so I got back to a good social level.

"How did you get those scars, Joyce?"

"Down at my Auntie's. There was a fight at the Con Club. The police said I can't talk about it."

"Ah, go on, Joyce."

I was a normal girl again. I'd say a sort of normal. That's all it ever could be. There was no more Yvonne and the Cinder Bank lot. No more proper social life. And there was the cover up. The constant lie and the constant worry that it would slip. A constant empty stomach feeling. More than this though. I was always pretending – simulating. Under it all I felt sick, tight-throated, confused.

School was alright. There was a blueprint to follow. I knew how to play the game with kids and teachers. The same, to a degree, with family stuff. But alone, and always underneath it all, was this sicky anxiety. Alone was the worst. Dreams were the worst. Dreams still are. The pills made me sick. Pretending made me sick. I was good at being alright.

They gave me pills to sleep. They gave me pills to eat with my breakfast. It normally took me a good hour or so to shake away the dreams. It would be in the dark green and brown of Saltwells. Lying on the wet ground. Yvonne straddled me. Sat on my chest. Knees pinning arms back. Hands reaching deep into mouth. Fingers searching down throat. Then slowly pulling out, like a fisherman reeling in a catch, a long, thick, matted tangle of hair. I'd wake choking. Unable to move. Drowning.

It's like guilt. You've got to find a way to shake it. To satisfy it. I had no way to shake it off. Just imagine going about your day to day, faking it every day, being normal, but all the time never settling. I thought about Yvonne all the time.

I don't know. I still don't. I wanted to get her. I wanted to hold her. I wanted to explain. I wanted her to explain. I was lost with it all. I couldn't stop thinking about her. We were queens of the gang.

162

Leather jackets, leaning against the gates of St Andrews churchyard. That little cough-giggle. Our half-smiles and the whispers. We ruled and did it with ease.

Rules and order helped. Helped settle things. I stuck to the rules of school, family and whatnot with strict and rigid steps. I obeyed and that helped. I was studious and dutiful and that helped. I was hard. Dad helped with the trigonometry and that helped. I set strict rules around myself and that helped, and if anyone made moves to undermine those rules they got it. That's why Tim got it those years later. He'd brought it back up. I'm not blaming him.

There was a girl called Diane at school. She said something to me on the hockey pitch. I can't even remember now but it made me unsteady. It bought the sickness up. Like I said, I knew how to play the game, so I finished her. I planted seeds. I was always good at it. Calculated and well sown seeds. I spread rumours. Diane was finished and the sickness subsided. The cover-up was safe. It happened to a few girls. I carried on. Soon enough it became instinct. The rules became a way of being. Habit, it's still there, I suppose. Sorry.

But before this. Before the rules and order and control, there was Yvonne. I couldn't shake her. I'd woken too many times, drowning and paralysed. She was stronger than me. She'd proven it. In some dreams we'd be in the darkness of the cinema. Alone. Staring at the screen. She'd take my hand and then came burning, pins and needles. Constant, building stabbing.

I was good at pretending, I knew the game. It didn't take long for the teachers to start loving me again.

"Great game, Joyce," Mr Reynolds said. "Best I've seen you. So alert. So commanding."

"Thank you, sir," I said. "I feel back to normal again now."

"Good. Mr Pritchard said the same too, Joyce."

It didn't take long for Dad to start taking the shield down. He'd been coming to the hockey games. I'd seen him chatting with Mr Reynolds. Seen them laughing together. It was over, almost. I asked Mom and Dad if I could go to see the cousins.

"I'm not so sure, Joyce," Mom said. We were out having Friday chips.

"Come on, she's doing much better," Dad said. "You said yourself. And it's only her cousins. It'll do her good."

"Just your cousins, eh Joyce? We're trusting you."

"Look at her grades. Look at the hockey results. Think about what Mr Pritchard said. She's okay. Just wants to see her cousins."

Then he turned to me quietly. "Remember what I said, Joyce? This is a point of trust. Keep on track."

And I did. I took the cousins off to Saltwells. Me and the cousins played games, I was lovely to them and they told Auntie and I was safe. But it was reconnaissance. I was spying. I'd take the cousins around Saltwells and teach them the tricks Dad had taught me. We hunted for eggs and went bramble picking and all that. Built wigwams. Played hunt the flag. I was tracking Yvonne.

Auntie had called home a few times and the cousins were happy.

"Is that right?" Mom spoke down the telephone. "I am glad ... that's good ... well, it's a difficult time when you're her age, isn't it? ... I think so too, it's done with ... yeah, her dad taught her all of that ... see you soon, Sis."

I went back to Netherton on a solo mission, I did it few times. I'd meet them for a few nights over a few weeks then just do one night, alone, with Yvonne in mind. I don't even know what I had planned. But you see, she was the issue. I'd been signed out of trouble now. School, family, all of that was alright. But there was that sickness. The constant thought of her that just sat there like pins and needles inside me. It was Yvonne. It needed confronting.

It took me a few attempts. I'd walked Saltwells, the churchyard, trekked the whole of Cinder Bank, Buffery Park. I went all over Netherton. But I got her. I went to the Outdoor at The Bull, where we'd got the jug of Mild that night we made friends. I heard her giggle. She'd been in the pub. Actually inside. And you've got to remember we were still children, really. I heard her giggle and saw her through the latch. It was only a split second but she looked different. Livelier. Grown up. She was in a dress and makeup. She was different. Yvonne was always confident, always a bit older than her years, but she'd moved from the Outdoor and into

165

the pub. It was too much and I ran off. I didn't go back to Netherton for a week. The dreams wouldn't let up.

The Dreams wouldn't let up. Yvonne needed confronting. I had to go back. I was still a girl, I didn't know what I was getting into. I didn't know how to do this undercover stuff. But Yvonne needed managing. I went back. I tied my hair back, slicked it back with Dad's Brylcreem. I wore black, trousers and top, two sizes too big, stolen from school's lost property. I looked silly.

Back at The Bull I hid near the privet bushes opposite the outdoor. I spied. I waited. There were a couple of times I saw Yvonne walk past the light of the latch. She looked different again. Older, cooler, glamorous. She giggled and waved at someone. A small glass in her hand. I saw her once more, just for a split second, with someone else. A woman. Odd. I saw her rest her hand on the shoulder of a woman. She held it there and smiled at her. That woman was odd. She was older than us, a proper adult. I was too far to see properly, but she was different, odd. You can quickly tell who isn't from Netherton, can't you? It was too much for me again. I ran off.

Michelle

Our Gem always said, "there's different degrees 'a bein' Black Country, ay there?"

We knew when someone wor a regular in Turner's. Knew when they wor from Netherton. I doh know if iss a look or aura or what. There's degrees 'a things, ay there? Some of us am more nether than others. I remember a bloke called Rob, used to come in from time to time with our Gem, 'e was probably a puff too. 'E was sound. Day look down on no one, talked to anyone, got 'is round in. But 'e wor from Netherton. 'E wor a worker like us, day 'ave things like Saltwells an' ruins under 'is skin. They took a while to warm to 'im for that.

Joyce

I spent another week waking with chokes and unable to move. With the itchy agony of my knuckle. I dressed up again. Brylcreemed my hair. Stared long and hard at the bathroom mirror. Told myself to be strong.

I went back to the outdoor. It was night but it was summer so the light lasted long enough. I hid behind the privet bush again. Waited. It seemed like ages. Just watching the latch, the light, the figures against it. I kept checking my watch – every five minutes was an hour. Then I spotted her. She walked past the glow of the outdoor, stood there for a few seconds. She laughed at someone. Smiled. Then I saw that odd woman. They faced each other for a moment. She put her hand on Yvonne's shoulder. Yvonne smiled. It was seconds but I took it all in as if they performed in slow motion, just for me. She touched Yvonne. Yvonne liked the touch. I stayed put. Hours passed. Just me, night time, the privet bush. Every now and then Yvonne would pass the latch, I saw them both a couple of times. That was all.

It was tough. I wasn't sure how to feel. I wanted to be in there with her, laughing, being cool, being with her. I wanted to confront her. Tell her what she'd done to me. Ask her to justify herself. Apologise to her. I wasn't sure how to feel but it swelled in me, those pins and needles, that sickness, that empty stomach groan. It was tough.

I think it must have been an hour or two before I heard her giggle again. Yvonne's giggle, outside. I held my breath. I watched Yvonne walking up the road. Got a good look at her this time. She looked cool, older than before. Strutting. She walked away from The Bull, turned around to look behind her, smiled as she faced forward again. She smiled that smile of hers – that cool, on the level, smile. Ten seconds later that woman followed. She was lanky, tall; older than us. She looked odd. Walked in a strange way. She smiled too. Her teeth were crooked, one was chipped. She walked off through the estate.

I held my breath. Counted to ten, followed. They went through the estate, past all the redbrick terraces. Up past St Andrew's. Down Lodge Hill. Past the reservoir. Slipped over the stile into Saltwells. It was dark now. I already knew I was too late for home. But I followed. Through the tarmac, trying to tread softly, keeping distance. Into the woods. It was almost pitch black in Saltwells. All the greens and browns had turned black, grey, blue. I followed. First Yvonne, then that odd woman, then me. Cutting through bracken, nettles, hawthorn. She was a proper adult, but me and Yvonne were still just kids, really. They didn't look fazed. I was. They looked assured, determined. I felt lost, but I followed. Off the path, past the bell pits, through scratching thickets. It was hard to see, hard to tread carefully. I think I saw them take each other's hands. But I followed.

They stopped at a little opening. A small circular patch of dead ground. They were side by side now. I think they held hands. The strange woman turned, resting her back against a fat old tree. It looked dead, hollow, brittle. Yvonne stepped towards her. They kissed.

Yvonne

I grab at tits, and nibble on neck. We kissed an' l pulled up 'er dress to get to 'er skin an' stick fingers in 'er knickers, kissed that wench, stroked and touched 'er. Fingered 'er.

I day know we'd been followed but I let the thought 'a Joyce play in me yed. "Er'd 'a cried a bit, I was 'er fust crush, 'an 'er day 'ave nothin' to cling it to, an' 'er wanted me to be 'ers but 'er day know the words to use in 'er own yed to figure it out properly. 'Er couln't figure it out, an' 'er'd said 'ow 'er liked things clean an' in theya place, day 'er?

I pinned that wench to the tree and ran lips all over 'er. Joyce 'ad started this, I suppose. 'Er'd med me queer. I pulled out the wench's tit an' sucked, nibbled.

169

Nipples, solid, pink.

Joyce 'ad kissed me. I got off just thinkin' 'er might 'ave sid us.

Joyce

I didn't know what was happening. I just squatted in the bracken, watching. I was angry, sad, and sorry. Full of that empty stomach sickness, dizzy with it all. And I felt that throbbing. Just the same as the night I tried to take Yvonne. I can feel it now as I'm telling you. I wanted Yvonne, wanted to possess her. I hated that woman. Straight away, as soon as I saw her with her wonky walk and weird face. I hated her. I hated Yvonne. But I couldn't turn away, I had to watch, and I felt that building, longing throb, and I hated myself for that. I was confused and afraid. I felt odd; all of it was odd. The woods filled with a mood. Like a gas leak filling a room. You could taste the mood. When I dream now, I dream of that mood – it has a smell, a weight. The smell of Saltwells.

Tim

That earthy rot that'd cling to your nails, like. That shit smell you doh want to smell but cor stop smellin', like. That mood. Like a hangover sickness, iss relief but iss vile. I thought about Dave. Honestly, it would'a bin the same for 'im. It's more than just first crush or first love though, ay it? It's the first time, an' first person it's alright to be queer with. Or you thought it was alright,

170

like. There was somethin' no one else'd understand, an' it'd bin broken. An' it was summat that day 'ave a name or a story like so many of these things do, so you doh know it's sacred, like, until it's done with. Honestly, we 'ad somethin'. Sometimes the somethin' comes too long after the event though, an' it's too late.

Michelle

Our Gem said the sem when 'er an' Hannah broke up.

"It ay just a broken 'eart, bab, iss loss, iss spoiled."

Joyce

I squatted in the bushes like a toad and watched them. Knees under chin. Back and thighs burning. I ignored the burn. Watched them loving each other. Can you understand? Then something happened, changed the mood. I heard footsteps. The two of them seemed to as well. I watched Yvonne pin the woman against the tree and saw both of their heads snap toward the sounds. They covered each other's mouths with their palms. Eyes wide. I stayed toad-like, flicking eyes from Yvonne and her lover to the sounds stepping the woods. I wanted to stand and I wanted to say something and I wanted to stay hidden and pull Yvonne away and witness it all. I wanted all those. The distinct sound of footsteps, closing in – thud on dry earth, crack against broken branches, dull hammer of clods kicked to dust, syncopated stomps of different weights of man, different sizes of boots, different gaits. Wood pigeons and ravens clapped wings away as these sounds increased. I watched them as each palm gripped the other's mouth, wild eyes squinting, then widening, limbs stiff and tense. I quickly looked around, head moving in sharp spasms. I couldn't feel my feet. The scar on my hand burned and my flesh goose-pimpled. I was not the only onlooker. I held my breath. I was not alone in following them. My hands became fists against the stems of bracken. The stem's skin broke under my grip and bled cool tears on to my hands. I held my breath. There was movement in the woods. I stayed still, squat, staring. I held my breath. Footsteps, a group of footsteps, closing in. My eyes twitched in snaps to and from the lovers and towards the footsteps. Then I froze. Five or six dim figures stepped out of the bushes, moved into the circle. They were calm. They were composed, regimented. I watched them close in. I don't remember it being rushed but it happened quickly. I stuck to my spot, sat in the brackens, close to the damp stench of the soil, night time dews kissing my face. Moths and midges darted and skipped the cold air. I held my breath. I was toad-like. The scar on my hand burned. Flesh goose-pimpled. A slight sweat covered my skin. And I thought about Mom and Dad and the cousins and school and the plans to go to America and mushroom picking and damson pickling and I couldn't look away and I held fast to the stems of the bracken. The men closed in. Not quickly, not slowly. Casual stepping. I saw Yvonne sprint. She'd turned for half a second, let go of the woman. She fled.

It was hard to see, it was dark. There would have been about six of them. Each with a big stick in their hand. They had rope with them. I'm sorry. They tied her up. They battered her. I did nothing. I'm sorry. I was a girl. They tied her up and I saw them take turns at bringing sticks down on to her. In the quiet of night, in the stillness of the woods. That thud and thump of them was horrific. I can hear it now. Like the sound of a cricket ball, dropped from a height, in an empty sports hall. I'm sorry. I did nothing. I was a girl. They hid her in the trunk of the tree. I'm sorry. I did nothing.

Tim

I asked 'er why she didn't tell anyone. I said someone was murdered. I told 'er she could've given a statement years later. You hear about it, doh ya? 'Er day come back to Lye. But 'er'd be alright, the bikers were bostin'.

I go over sometimes, to the Wych-Elm. It's marked with me an' Dave. We're part of the echo.

Joyce

I don't think these dreams will stop. That empty stomach feeling won't either. I didn't do anything. I'm sorry. But I couldn't. I won't be able to stop covering up in some way or other, I'll never lose it. I don't blame Yvonne for any of it. It was before all of this, before there was an *Us* we could stick together with. Before there was an *Other* to name in any of us.

There was part of me that wanted to keep Yvonne safe. Keep myself safe. I knew I'd end up explaining things to the police again. Netherton's a small place, it'd get around who saw what, it'd put us all in the firing line. Put me in the firing line again. There was part of me that just carried on building this front – this shield – pushing it to the back helped with that. I know someone died. I've told you and I've told it once. I won't tell it again.

Anon

Wid sid 'er before. 'Er was more mon than wench. We wor 'avin that. We wor perfect but thass against God that is. An' that night wi' the young girl – Niall an' Ben knew 'er. Weem together ay we? Long hot hours down Roundoak – weem together. Suppin in the Bull – together. St Andrews or the Methodists on a Sundee – together. Wid sid 'er before. We wor 'avin' that. Alfred took the lead. Grabbed the cricket bat 'e'd bin given at the four counties, 'e'd 'elped to build it. 'E shut the bar early an' we followed 'em. Dirty devil wench.

Bella

It must have been quick or I must have faded in and out. Memory is difficult. You closed in. She ran. You came for me. Better to get one properly than chase the other and risk losing both. You closed in. You were silent. I must have faded in and out.

I taste the iron of my blood. Count three loose teeth. Wrists roped – I seethe. Then thump. Crack. The sound of mallets working dry clods. Thump – six, seven, eight. Nothing.

12

Michelle

We cor tell no one. Thass the echo that clings to Saltwells woods. Iss never safe. Thass the place that sits on the edge 'a our estates, next to the rusts and rots of our forges. That in-between place full 'a ancient fossils and limestone, full 'a swampy bell pits. Stuck theya with Merry Hill shopping centre on one side, an' our Nether Town on the other. Iss framed by the res, the red-bricks, the industrial estate. Iss at the 'eart of us. Bella is too, ay 'er? An' that rotten Wych-Elm, ay it? Iss the twisted root of our heartland.

I told our Gem all about it. 'Er couln't believe it.

"I know iss bin tough for loads of us lot over the years, bab, but thass fuckin' awful," 'er said. "Meks sense too though, doh it? Bella an' the Wych-Elm 'as

177

'ung around us all 'round 'ere. Thass the weight 'a 'ate, that is. Thass the weight 'a guilt an' lies."

Our Gem was right. We all try to kip it at the back of our 'eads, bury it like poor Bella, but thass where it festers, ay it? An' all them festerin' feelins, they all come from us, an' they all infiltrate us, an' we all tek a bit away an' we all add a bit. An' weem all the cause an' weem all the symptom an' we cor gerr'away from the spreadin'.

After I told our Gem, 'er said we should goo an' see it.

"We oughta goo find Bella," 'er said. "I dunno, put some flowers down or summat."

So I called Tim an' 'e agreed to tek us. 'E wor scared an' 'e always loved another chance to 'old court. It 'elped 'im too a bit, I think. So we met at the visitor's centre an' 'e took us in. Through the dirty paths, lined with bushes, nettles an' trees. Cuttin' through a patch 'a 'awthorn, past the bell pits an' bits 'a jagged limestone, along a dirt line where a few strange sorts 'ad trod before. Then we sid it. We cut out 'a thickets into a wide circular area, all dead an' brown, 'cept the tree. It was massive. I dropped to my knee. This fat, crusty trunk squatted in the centre, iss wide span 'a windin' branches twistin' out, droopin'. Dead but still 'ere.

I 'eard Tim sniff, wipe 'is face an' walk forward. Gem stepped forward too – 'er touched the trunk an' shook 'er 'ead. She left the flowers at the base. Tucked 'em under a few roots that'd pierced the dirt and spiralled around each other. Then 'er moved back. Tim stayed for a few minutes. We 'eard 'im sniffin, 'eard 'is 'ard breathin'.

"'E's 'avin' a cry, ay 'e?" our Gem said.

On his knees, right up against the tree, back to us, 'e was there for about five minutes. Sniffin', breathin', 'e's body shekin' a bit. When 'e moved back we saw it. In the bark, etched: *Dave 4 Tim 4 eva.*

I remember drivin' up from The Delph towards Cradely, an' we were stopped at the lights at the top 'a Quarry Bank. Tony was wi' me an' 'e'd pointed it out. It ay nothin' 'cept a border between a couple 'a places that ay proper towns anyroad. Tomatoes growin' out 'a the tarmac.

Tony called me a wik after that.

"Ya know them tomatoes wid sin, bab? I went back to pick 'em. They wor tomatoes like I've 'ad before!"

I day know what they was. No one down Turner's believed us.

"Them like tomatoes but they ay right. Them really sweet, too sweet. An' them really sour, too sour. Sweet pulp and sour skin – or was it sweet outside, and sour within?"

Bella

You call me Bella. I am always here. Lurking. I am just out of sight. Just out of reach. I am the mar. I am the foxy infraction. Never living, never dead. A shade that germs into and out of you.

Acknowledgements

Bella is based on my PhD research conducted at the University of Wolverhampton - thanks to the Centre for Transnational and Transcultural Research, the Faculty of Arts and School of Humanties.

I'm hugely grateful to Ben Colbert, Jackie Pieterick, Aidan Byrne, Luke Kennard, Niall Griffiths and Anthony Cartwright. Special thanks to Paul McDonald for his support and friendship.

I'm indebted to Tracey and Phil at Wild Pressed Books for their warmth, effort and time – thank you for taking a chance on this odd little book of mine.

About the Author

R. M. Francis is a writer from Dudley. He completed his PhD at the University of Wolverhampton for a project titled Queering the Black Country and graduated from Teesside University for his Creative Writing MA.

He's the author of four poetry chapbooks, Transitions (The Black Light Engine Room Press, 2015), Orpheus (Lapwing Publications, 2016), Corvus' Burnt-Wing Love Balm and Cure-All (The Black Light Engine Room Press, 2018) and Lamella, (Original Plus, 2019).

9 781916 489677